Harold and the Hot Rod

Hound's Glenn Series · Book Two

Tonton Jim
E. Felix Lyon

Dayton Publishing LLC
P. O. Box 1521
Solana Beach, CA 92075
858-254-2959
publisher@daytonpublishing.com

ISBN-13: 978-0-9893290-3-3

Also by Tonton Jim and E. Felix Lyon:

Max and the Lowrider Car
Hound's Glenn Series • Book One

Available from **amazon.com, barnesandnoble.com,** and independent booksellers worldwide (find one near you at **indiebound.org**)

To the illustrator, E. Felix Lyon, and the editor/ publisher, Linnea Dayton, without whom the Hound's Glenn books would not have been possible. And to the wise and wonderful children I've been fortunate to know.
— Tonton Jim

To the natural world, and to all who take the time to appreciate its beauty and magic.
— E. Felix Lyon

We are grateful to the artists and writers of the storybooks, the comic books, the Sunday funnies, and the cartoons of television and movies that children have enjoyed for decades. The happiness and smiles they gave us have lasted a lifetime. We hope that for centuries to come children will smile and laugh at their everyday silliness and enchanting fantasy.

Contents

The Young Ones

Max

Theena

NicNac

Edgar

The Teens

Harold

Wil

Chapter One

Current Events

Life in Hound's Glenn had pretty much returned to normal after the invasion of the birds from Leggyville. Hardly any feathers were still blowing around town, and the old-timers again played their Saturday afternoon concerts in the town square. There were now four low-riding customized cars— Mr. L. Lobo's original Numero Uno, a low-riding coupe belonging to Max's big brother, Wil, and two others made from the roundy cars collected on that first trip to Big Pig City. And more were being built in Mr. L. Lobo's garage and auto-body shop.

Most of us might say, "Hoo, doggies! Our four young ones — the three wolf cubs and one pup — have had more than enough adventure for one year." But sometimes adventures come upon you one right after another.

After the road trip and the perturbed-bird visit, summer started as it always had for the young ones. First, two weeks of absolute freedom...and then some summer school. Oh, but those first fourteen days of no-waiting-for-the-school's-out-bell, no homework, and no anything they didn't feel like doing — those were wonderful days. Mornings in the park they mostly played classic doggie games like Hare and Hounds. Then there was lunch at one of their houses — their parents took turns feeding the cubs and pup because the four of them didn't like to part ways, even for lunch. When it was Theena's turn for lunch, her father, Mr. L. Lobo, would stop work in his auto shop and treat them all to a meal at a nearby diner. All of them always ordered tofu sausages on long rolls, something they called "sausage sandwiches" (you didn't think the canines would call them by another name, did you?).

For our graduated fifth-graders, summer school this year promised to be more than just a little interesting, because this year, they would finally be able to attend Ms. Chienne's Summer Science Camp. With their bright and curious minds, they had enjoyed her lessons from the very first day. It was now the fourth week of the summer program, and on this already hot morning Ms. Chienne (Max pronounced it "chain") stood at the door to welcome her students. When all were inside, she moved to the front of the classroom and held up her long ears, which was her signal for the class to become quiet and pay attention.

Ms. Chienne

"Little canines," she said, "the Summer Science Fair is only two weeks

2

from today. So, if you have something planned, or if you want help choosing a project, please come see me after class."

Max, Edgar, and NicNac grinned at one another. Led by the creative mind of Max, they had won first prize at last year's regular-school science fair, and they planned to do it again this summer. Max noticed that Theena was quiet, thinking about something.

"And now, little canines, I have some wonderful news for you," Ms. Chienne was saying. "After our science fair, for this year's Dog Days outing — our day of fun and cooling off during the very hottest part of the summer — we are going...," and she paused to tease them a bit, *"to the water slides in River Otter City!"*

Ms. Chienne allowed the class to howl and bark with delight for a few seconds. Then she held up her ears again, for quiet attention.

"Class, let's begin the day," she said. "For today's science-in-current-events report, NicNac will tell us about this weekend's bridge collapse near Piglet Town."

NicNac stood in front of the class, smiled, and showed them the article he had cut out of the Sunday paper. "Saturday, because of too many critters swaying all together at once on the bridge, the Piglet Town Bridge started vibrating so hard that it broke apart and fell into the river, along with many critters."

"Was anyone hurt?" asked Manny, who was still the newest cub in town.

3

"No, but many piglets were…," and here NicNac paused to read from the article, "'severely dampened to the point of wetness.'"

"What were so many piglets doing on the bridge?" asked Jolie, a pup in the third row.

"The sway," said NicNac.

"No, I mean, why were so many of them on the bridge at the same time?"

NicNac looked down at his article, and everyone waited until he found the answer. "Oh, it was the day of the annual Piglet Pageant, and they were sway-marching along, carrying their pageant queen over the bridge to the festival."

"Was she hurt?" asked Theena.

"Umm, no, but," said NicNac, and then he read on, "'she was the first to make a big splash. Some suspect that the large pageant queen wasn't really a piglet at all, but a full-grown sow who had failed to make it to the finals in last year's contest.'" He held up the clipping, which included an amazing color photo of the accident in progress.

"What's the name of the river the bridge went across?" asked a cub.

"The Iffy River," replied NicNac, "the mighty Iffy River."

"Thank you, NicNac, for your report," said Ms. Chienne.

"Yep, the mighty Iffy River," continued NicNac. "It might just keep rolling, that mighty Iffy River."

"Thank you, NicNac," said Ms. Chienne.

"Roll on, you mighty Iffy River," said NicNac, who looked like he was lost in a daydream.

"You may sit down, NicNac," said Ms. Chienne. As he strolled back to his seat, NicNac kept saying, almost singing, "Roll on, roll on, you mighty Iffy River."

"Ms. Chienne," asked Theena, as NicNac finally sat down, "doesn't the main highway to All Critters City go over that bridge?"

"I think you're right, Theena. I guess everyone will have to take The Long Way if they want to get there.

A newspaper clipping includes a photo of the Piglet Town Bridge collapse, taken by a passenger in a passing boat.

Let's look at the map." She pulled down a map in front of the whiteboard, pointed to Hound's Glenn, and traced a path to AC City on a mostly dirt road that seemed to wander all over the place. "Why, that would take two weeks, at least."

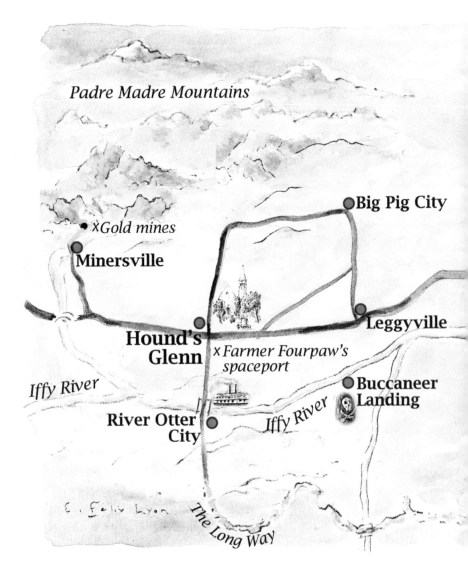

"Ms. Chienne, couldn't you just go down the river on a boat?" asked Edgar.

"Hmm," said Ms. Chienne, "that river does flow to the ocean and to AC City, but I don't think these days there are many riverboats still steaming up and down the…"

"The mighty Iffy River, Ms. Chienne?" asked NicNac.

"Yes, NicNac — the mighty Iffy River."

*A*fter school our four young friends walked down Main Street toward the candy store to buy some ice-cold pupsicles on this hot afternoon. Max, Edgar, and NicNac talked mostly about the upcoming science fair. Max's plan was to build a model of Main Street with little metal cars and trucks stuck in a traffic jam because of a broken-down car. Towering over the buildings they would place cranes with magnets hanging down, to pick up broken-down cars and swing them over to an auto repair shop.

Max turned to Theena. "And we can put your father's name on the auto repair shop, only we might have to make his sign bigger so people can read it on the little model building."

"He'd like that," she said.

"Of course, you can join our science team and help us," said Max.

"Thank you, but I think I'm going to do my own project."

"What are you going to do?" asked Edgar.

"I'm thinking of building a steam engine," she replied.

"A steam engine?" said Max. "Does anyone use steam engines anymore?"

"Well, they do in steamboats," Theena said. "Anyway, Pop can help me and it'll be fun."

As they finished their rapidly melting pupsicles, they walked out the back door of the candy store and crossed the alley to Mr. L. Lobo's garage and auto-body shop. The three wolf cubs and the hound pup entered the garage, and right away their eyes focused on the Too Tall Coupe parked in the center. Edgar's older brother, Harold, was standing next to it. The old-school hounds of Hound's Glenn preferred these cars made by the Too Tall Car Company. But they were too boxy to customize into roundy low-riding cars, so Theena was curious as to what this car was doing in her father's customizing body shop.

"Are you going to work on that coupe, Pop?" she asked.

The four friends find Harold in Mr. L. Lobo's garage, standing next to a Too Tall Coupe.

"Harold wants me to," he answered.

"Did you buy that old wreck?" Edgar asked his brother.

"Yep, I bought it from Lonesome Rodney," Harold replied.

Indeed, the young ones could read Rodney's name painted on the side of the coupe — the first half of it, anyway, because the letters "R," "O," and "D" were on the open door that faced them. When Harold closed the door, they could see the whole name, "RODNEY." The lonesome hound had been desperate for everyone to know his name and maybe shout out a "hello" to him.

"Yeah, the body work I can do," Mr. L. Lobo was saying to Harold. "No problem." He stroked his chin and ran his paw along the coupe's boxy body. "Just bring it back when you finish your work on the chassis and the engine."

"It's not going to be like Numero Uno?" asked Theena.

"No, Harold wants to make this coupe into a fast racing car," said her father.

The four young ones looked to Harold. Before the bird invasion, most every canine in town thought the always cheerful Harold just a bit...well, there's a word for it, but polite canines never used it.

"I'm gonna replace this four-banger engine with a truck's V8," explained Harold. "And to keep that power to the ground, I'm gonna replace these skinny tires and wheels with much fatter ones."

10

"Hmm," said Mr. L. Lobo. "If you do that, then we'll need to modify these wheel wells."

"Yep, and throw away the engine hood — won't need that at all," said Harold.

By now, the young ones were wide-eyed with wonder as they looked at Harold. Edgar had to ask his brother, "Why are you doing all this?"

Harold smiled and said simply, "I want to race it."

"It'll be a new type of car," said Wil, who worked in Mr. L. Lobo's shop and had just finished straightening up the tool cabinet.

"Sure won't be like Pop's customized roundy cars," said Theena.

"Sure won't," said Max. "What are you going to call this new type of car?"

Harold just stroked his muzzle and shook his head.

"Boy, it sure is hot," said NicNac.

"*Hot* is a good word for this car," said Wil.

"No, I mean it's hot today," said NicNac.

"Yeah, 'hot,'" said Mr. L. Lobo. "But 'hot' what?"

"How about 'hot hound'?" suggested Harold. When no one said anything, he added, "I'll think on it some."

"Wait a doggone minute," shouted out Edgar. "Just where in the doggone world are you going to race it?"

"AC City — you know, All Critters City," said Harold without taking his eyes off the Too Tall Coupe.

"There's going to be a custom car show there," said Wil as he handed a flyer to his little brother. Max read

11

the information aloud, "Custom car show…car racing …big prizes…" He wondered if his brother and Harold knew about the bridge collapse. If so, he wondered what they were planning to do about getting to AC City. If they didn't know, he didn't want to be the one to tell them.

"Well, I'll be heading home," said Harold. "Want a ride, little bro?"

"No thanks," said Edgar, "I'll be home later."

"Okay, see ya." Harold left the shop, got into his father's Too Tall Coupe, and waved good-bye. Then he put both hands firmly on the wheel and drove away.

"You could get home quicker by running," said NicNac to Edgar.

"He's not a fast driver," said Edgar.

"He did alright on the road trip," said Theena.

"We weren't racing then — except when we had to hightail it out of Leggyville," said Max.

"He's the most careful driver in town. Everyone says so," said Edgar.

"Boy-oh-boy — Harold, a race car driver," said NicNac.

As the four friends watched Harold drive away down the alley, they caught sight of the eight-hundred-pun gorilla exiting the back door of the nightclub called The Room, and coming toward them up the alley. Max whispered to the others, "I heard he finally got fired from The Room."

Upon seeing the young ones, the gorilla smiled and said, "I say there, cubs and pup, I'm of the mind that you would all greatly enjoy one of my classic witticisms."

"Oh, no thanks!" they all shouted, except NicNac, who still liked the gorilla's old and often repeated jokes. The gorilla sighed and kept walking.

"I wonder what's he going to do now." said Max.

"I don't know," said Edgar, "but he's got a suitcase, and he's headed in the direction of the bus station."

NicNac turned around and shouted, "Good luck, Mr. Gorilla!"

The gorilla turned his head, smiled, and raised his top hat to wave good-bye.

Chapter Two

Water Slides and Steamboats

$\mathcal{T}$he day of the Summer Science Fair arrived. The model Main Street that the two cubs and pup had built looked pretty much like Hound's Glenn's real Main Street. The three towering cranes looked almost real. The metal model cars made the traffic jam look very real. The only problem was the pedestrians on the sidewalks. You see, Max, Edgar, and NicNac hadn't been able to find little plastic canine figures, so they used little metal ones. And every time they operated a crane near the sidewalk, its magnetic grabber would pick up four or five of the metal canines and leave them swinging over Main Street.

"NicNac, stop picking up the pedestrians," whispered Max as the science fair judges looked down at the model.

The judges stroked their muzzles, made entries in their notebooks, and moved on to the next science project, Theena's. As Max watched them walk away, he had a sad feeling that his team wasn't going

14

to win even a second prize. He turned to Edgar and NicNac to express his worries, but they had wandered off to join the crowd around Theena's little steam engine.

"Not so long ago, steam engines were used to power tractors," Theena said as she pointed at her display board and its picture of a steam-powered tractor. "And, of course, they also powered the riverboats that carried travelers and freight."

She turned away from the board and pointed to her huffing and puffing steam engine. "This boiler is heated by this kerosene-fueled burner. When the water gets hot enough, it turns to steam. And just like the steam in a tea kettle, it comes out of the boiler rather fast. But in a steam engine the force of the steam pushes the piston back. My steam engine has a single-action piston and is helped in completing its cycle by this heavy wheel, which is called a *flywheel.*"

She again faced her display board and pointed to a picture of a river steamboat. "But steamboats, being large and heavy, require double-acting pistons and huge boilers in order to turn their big paddlewheels."

"You know, Theena," said Principal Hurler, who was one of the science fair judges, "River Otter City has a riverboat port, and if I remember rightly, there's an old steamboat that docks there sometimes. I think it's called the *Iffy Queen.*"

"Yes," said Theena. "I'm hoping to see it when we go there for Dog Days next week."

"Ah, steamboats," said one of the other judges, "My mother and father used to take riverboats when they wanted to go down to AC City. Oh, the stories they used to tell me..."

"Mine, too," added the other judge.

"Well done, Theena," said Principal Hurler. "Fellow judges, are we agreed?"

They happily nodded their heads, and so Principal Hurler attached the blue ribbon with the big number "1" to Theena's display board. Everyone clapped their paws — including Max, Edgar, and NicNac.

Principal Hurler awards First Prize to Theena's steam engine project.

With the fun of the science fair over and done and Summer Science Camp winding down, it was time for the trip to the water slides. The bus trip to nearby River Otter City the following Monday didn't take long. The road went along as the crow flies south and crested a hill, and from the hilltop everyone looked down at the Iffy River and the town where the fun-loving river otters lived.

"That's it?" asked Theena. "It doesn't look like a city. It looks more like a small town."

"It *is* a small town," said Ms. Chienne. "But the otters didn't like what the initials of River Otter Town spelled, so they changed Town to City, and now they're pretty pleased with themselves."

Indeed, the young ones could read the billboard welcoming them to the river town:

Welcome to
RIVER OTTER CITY
Where you'll have a ROC'ing good time!

As you probably already know, river otters love to play, and they especially love to slide down a muddy river bank into the cool water. When their riverboat port had begun to fail and fade away after the bridge was built downstream, they made the wise decision to build a water slide park. Now their town attracted money-spending critters, the otters continued to have fun, and the old riverboat

17

piers — well, they just kept on rotting away. In fact, painted on an old warehouse by the piers were the faded words,

Welcome to the port of
R. O. T.

But few saw that old welcoming sign. The road into town led right down the Main Street, and that led right to the water slide park, complete with picnic grounds and snack bars that served any critter's preferred food. Once in the parking lot, the buses and cars quickly emptied out. The slides were soon filled with howling happy pups and cubs (and some of the grownups), and the hot weather of Dog Days was forgotten.

Theena, at the top of the chute and about to slide down to the water, paused and glanced down the river. Not too far down the river bank she spied the old steamboat.

Behind Theena were three young river otters.

"Don't wait," said the first.

"Don't hesitate," said the second.

"Don't be a locked gate," said the third.

"Sorry," said Theena. "I was just looking at the old riverboat. You go ahead."

"Thanks," said the first as he dove head-first onto the slide.

"Go take a close look," said the second as he followed his friend into the chute.

"Ask Pegleg — he'll row you there," said the third. He pointed down to an otter in a rowboat and then leapt onto the slide.

Looking where he had pointed, Theena saw a gray-muzzled river otter in a sailor's cap. She decided she would go see the steamboat close-up, so she started that journey with one step, a slide down the chute, and a splash into the cool water. Instead of swimming to shore, she dogpaddled to where the rowboat lay half in the water and half on the shore.

"Hello," she called out to the elderly river otter. "Are you Mr. Pegleg?"

"Well, hello, young wolfette," he said. "Pegleg I be. Able-bodied river-boater at your service. But you swim just fine — you wouldn't be needing a boat, would you?"

At the top of the water slide, one of the young river otters points out Pegleg and his boat near the entrance to the river.

"The river otters on the slide said you could row me down to the steamboat," she said as she walked onto the shore. "And maybe you could introduce me to the captain."

Pegleg

"Old Captain Blighwater? Sure, I could do that. He and I are old shipmates."

"Great! Will you wait here for me? I have to go tell my teacher."

Theena ran off to find Ms. Chienne. In a few minutes she came hurrying back with Harold and Max.

"My teacher said I needed to bring along Harold," Theena explained. "And Max said he wanted to come too. Is that alright?"

"To be sure, my little wolfette. That's what I'm here for." said Pegleg, and he pointed to a sign on a nearby post. It read:

Rowing Lessons
Free for park guests

"My name is Theena, Mr. Pegleg," she said, hoping he would stop calling her "wolfette."

"Right pretty name you have. Theena it is," said Pegleg. "And just calls me Pegleg. No 'mister' about it. Climb aboard and sit on that back seat there. Max, you too. Harold, you sit there in the middle and face rearwards like me. You're going to row."

"Gee, I've never rowed a boat before," said Harold as he stepped aboard and put his paws on the ends of two oars.

"Nothing to it, grommet," Pegleg said with a wink to Theena and Max.

Harold did splash his oars quite a bit while rowing, and sometimes on the stroke he had one oar in the water and one oar in the air, which caused the boat to come around in a half circle. Pegleg wasn't rowing at all, but relaxing in the front, smoking his pipe and calling out advice once in awhile.

"I'll make a river-critter out of you yet," said Pegleg. "And then, perhaps the captain will take you on as crew."

"Is Captain Blighwater a nice animal?" asked Theena.

"He's not like us otters, but he's alright for a giant toad. And as a captain he's stern but fair-minded."

"I've never met a toad before," said Theena. "Are toads good river-boaters?"

"Not as good as us river otters," Pegleg replied. "But they make good captains — mostly because they're very serious-looking and because they're very good at croaking orders and commands."

Something had been on Max's mind since he first met Pegleg, and now seemed like a good time to satisfy his curiosity. "Why are you called Pegleg?" he asked. "You have all your limbs and paws — I mean, I don't see a peg leg."

"Oh, a few years back, in a game of poker, I won a peg leg from a pirate who collects them."

"A pirate!" exclaimed Max and Theena.

"Yep. A puma river pirate by the name of Casanova Cugat," said Pegleg. "He isn't just half-bad, that Cugat. He's twice as worse. He is, by anyone's reckoning, the worst pirate in the history of this here river."

Theena and Max really wanted to ask more about this fearfully bad pirate, but they were now close to the riverboat, and Pegleg called out, "Ahoy, the *Iffy Queen!* Permission to come aboard!"

On the upper deck, a toad in a captain's hat looked down at them. His wide mouth made a stern expression, and he looked as if he were displeased with something, or everything. But he said simply, "Permission granted."

Two river otters paused in their swabbing of the deck, took the lines Pegleg tossed up from the rowboat, and secured the boat next to a ship's ladder. They helped Theena and Max up to the deck and then Pegleg scampered up the ladder.

Captain Blighwater came down to greet them. "Welcome aboard," he said to Theena and Max.

They each said "thank you" in return, and then they turned to watch Harold struggle aboard — the otters had gone back to swabbing the deck. Once on board, Harold smiled broadly, stuck out his paw to shake with the captain, and said, "Pleased to meet you, Captain Bilgewater."

"*Bligh*water," said the captain sternly, fixing a toad-eyed glare upon poor Harold. "It rhymes with *high* water — if you're a poetic sort of chap."

"Captain Blighwater, we wanted to see your riverboat," said Theena. "And I especially wanted to see the steam engines."

"Ah, well now, I'm always pleased to show off the old girl. She isn't as grand as some of the old

From the second deck, Captain Blighwater grants permission to come aboard the Iffy Queen.

floating palaces, but she's a stout boat, and in her day she was as fast as any boat on the river."

"My teacher said there aren't many riverboats left on the river," said Max.

"Yes, that's true. And that is very fortunate for me," the captain said. "What with the Piglet Town Bridge out of service and with so few riverboats to transport needed supplies up and down the river valley, I have been making quite a tidy sum of money lately. A very tidy sum, indeed."

Tidy sum

He pointed to the wide opening behind him and said, "Now here, as you can see, is where the *cargo* is stored. It *holds* quite a bit of cargo, and so we call it the *cargo hold*."

Harold looked inside and said, "It sure is big. I'll bet you could fit a couple of cars in here."

"That we have done on occasion," said the captain.

"Hey, Harold," said Max, "if you didn't feel like driving The Long Way, you could put your race car in here and cruise all the way to AC City."

"Hum, yeah, maybe," Harold replied, smiling at the thought. "Kind of funny, though — a fast car on a slow boat."

Again Captain Blighwater glared at Harold, who began to mumble, "Sorry, meaning no disrespect to your boat, which is probably, most certainly, very fast for a steamboat..."

24

Whether the Captain was satisfied with the apology or not, he didn't show it in his expression, which remained stern as he continued his tour. "Now, this main deck also is where the boilers and pistons are located," the captain said and then turned to face the two young ones. But Theena and Max had already discovered the gleaming brass of the engines. Theena pointed to one of the pistons and shouted back to the captain, "Are those double-acting pistons?"

Captain Blighwater arched an eyebrow and said, "Yes, those are that. Know something about steam engines, do you?"

Max peeked inside one of the boiler furnaces. "This must get super-hot."

"It certainly does," said the captain. "Steam engines can be quite dangerous."

They left the engine room and went to the rear of the boat, where the captain showed them the paddlewheel that was turned by the steam engines to propel the boat. They climbed up the stairs to the second deck, and he showed them a passenger room, or *cabin,* and then the dining hall, which he called a *saloon.* He finished the tour with a look around the third deck and even inside the pilothouse.

After letting Theena, Harold, and Max sit in his pilot's chair, he asked Max, as the young wolf gripped the ship's wheel, "Do you like the feel of the wheel? Are you already dreaming of becoming a riverboat captain?"

"Not exactly, Captain Blighwater," Max said hesitantly. "I sort of thought I would invent a space ship and fly into outer space."

"Flying!" exclaimed the captain. "Flying is for the birds. Get it? Flying is for the birds? I tell you — sometimes I can really tell a zinger."

The canines laughed softly, to be polite. They knew the rules. As they descended to the main deck, Theena asked the captain, "Where are you headed next? Are you going down the river to AC City?"

"Not yet," he said. "First I have to go up the river to Minersville and pick up a small, but very important, secret cargo. Mum's the word. And then it's down the river to AC City, but with a nearly empty cargo hold, I'm afraid. This time of the year, most of the shipping is up the river, not down. But that'll give me time to stop and visit my brother in the delta. I need to pay him back, so I'll be taking along my tidy sum of money. But mum's the word about that."

The young ones and Harold thanked the captain and climbed into the rowboat. Pegleg came around the corner — he had been goofing off with the two otter deckhands, who should have been swabbing the decks — and he, too, climbed down into the rowboat. Harold, still splashing water with the oars, rowed the boat back to the water slide park.

Chapter Three

Spaceport and River Cruise

$\mathcal{A}$ few days later Harold finished the engine work on his race car, and he wanted to try it out.

"Where are you going to test-drive it?" asked Edgar, who was watching Harold do a final adjustment to his carburetors in their parents' driveway.

"For sure, not in town," said Harold as he opened the carburetor barrels with his paw to make the engine roar.

"Well, yeah, I kind of guessed you wouldn't do it here...," said Edgar.

"I was kind of thinking about Farmer Fourpaw's spaceport landing strip," said Harold as he stopped the engine. "I'll go give him a call, and I'll call Wil and, for sure, Mr. L. Lobo. They'll want to come, too."

Farmer Fourpaw's spaceport landing strip had never been used by space ships, landing or taking off. After a night's dream — some say a night*mare* — he built it for the expected arrival of the spacemen. He had never tried building a spaceship for himself, probably because he hadn't the foggiest idea of how to, and definitely because flying machines (except for hot air balloons) were forbidden everywhere in this continent of animals — the birds wouldn't allow them. When the farmer explained to the local critters that the long runway was meant solely for the landing of spaceships and their spacemen, his neighbors shook their heads, and many of them also angrily shook their paws at him.

"Spacemen?" the grumpy animals grumbled to the farmer.

"It's bad enough we have to share this planet with humans..."

"To invite more people from another planet is just plain insane..."

But the pups and cubs loved the idea of visitors from outer space, and sometimes, daydreaming, they searched the twilight sky in the direction of the farm and its landing strip. Teenage hounds and wolves sometimes drove there, parked, and waited for something or someone to land — or so they claimed. Other than that, the mile-long runway sat unused.

Wil and Max were the first to arrive at Harold's house. They climbed out of Wil's custom coupe with the flames painted on the front and walked over to the driveway.

"You sure you've got her ready for a test drive, Harold?" Wil asked as he walked around the car.

"Yep, it's all done except the paint," said Harold. Mr. L. Lobo had made all the body modifications, but he hadn't painted it yet. In order to save money, Harold decided to do all the painting prep work himself. Most of that work was complete. Just the driver's door, which still had "ROD" on it, remained to be sanded.

"Do you think it's fast?" Max asked Edgar.

"It must be," said Edgar. "I've heard the engine roar, and full-throttle it's real loud."

Mr. L. Lobo and Theena drove up in Numero Uno but didn't get out. He called out, "Did Farmer Fourpaw say it's okay to use his runway?"

"Yep," said Harold with a broad smile.

"Okay, then. Lead the way," shouted Mr. L. Lobo.

Harold and Edgar climbed into the race car, and Wil and Max got back into Wil's car. All eyes were on Harold as he backed the car out of the driveway and into the street. He revved up the engine to a fearful noise, and then he let it idle down to a soft rumble. He put it into first gear, and the car slowly reached the speed limit, which on this residential street was 25 miles per hour. Wil put his car just behind Harold's. Mr. L. Lobo came up last of all.

By and by, the three-car convoy arrived at the farm. Harold stopped his car at one end of the broad runway, and the others parked off to the side. Farmer Fourpaw was waiting for them in his pickup truck.

He came over to greet them and to say, "I wanted to see what use you had for my runway. My neighbor,

Ol' Blue, kept telling me I was crazy to build it. But if you've got a good use for it — well, that'll be mighty pleasing to see."

Harold revved up the engine to a loud roar. The others noticed that instead of forming his usual cheerful smile, his lips were pressed tightly together, and his eyes had narrowed to slits. Suddenly the rear tires spun and squealed. His coupe rocketed forward and sped down the track.

"Hoo, doggies…" said Farmer Fourpaw. Everyone else was speechless.

They watched as Harold slowed at the far end of the runway and then whipped the car around, drifting the rear tires, until the car pointed back toward them. Again the engine roared, and in just seconds Harold

Harold test-drives his car on Farmer Fourpaw's landing strip.

arrived in front of them. Again he forced the car to drift around in a U-turn.

"Wow, I didn't know your brother could drive like that," said Max.

"Neither did I," said Edgar.

Harold revved up the engine, this time even louder than before. But then in a cloud of smoke and with a muffled boom, the engine blew. That is to say, he had cranked the engine up too high, some of the engine parts broke, and the engine died.

Concerned, everyone came over to the driver's window. Harold turned to them with his usual cheerful smile.

"Winkle-ringles, I guess that red line on the tachometer really *does* mean something."

"That's a real shame, Harold," said Mr. L. Lobo.

"Yeah," said Wil. "Can you fix it before we have to leave for AC City?"

Harold looked thoughtful for a few seconds, then shook his head. "Nope. I've got the spare parts, but it'll take me a few days — at least three — to fix it, and you fellas have to start the long drive the morning after tomorrow."

"It's a doggone shame the Piglet Town Bridge is out," said Wil.

Max and Theena looked at each other.

"Here's an idea," said Max.

"You can put your race car on Captain Blighwater's riverboat," said Theena.

$\mathcal{A}$s Mr. L. Lobo and Theena towed Harold's car back to the shop, "Pop," said Theena, "we can tow Harold's car to the steamboat, and we can put your car on board also. That way Numero Uno won't get damaged from driving all those miles on that terrible Long Way. Once we're on the river, you can spend all your time detailing the car and writing your thank-you speech for when you win the Grand Prize. And Harold can fix his racer."

Mr. L. Lobo noticed the "we" in his daughter's plan.

"And Pop," Theena continued in a rush, "did you know, All Critters City is the safest city for any kind of young animal. It's their tolerance laws — the strictest in the land — *the* strictest. And Ms. Chienne says that everyone ought to visit AC City sometime. It's a very educational experience."

Mr. L. Lobo just nodded his head without taking his eyes off the road.

Meanwhile, in the Loupin household, Max could tell that his sales pitch wasn't exactly winning over his parents. It didn't help that his triplet little sisters giggled and whispered to each other all through his plea. Wil, of course, had already obtained permission. Mr. and Mrs. Loupin thought the trip would be an excellent learning experience for Wil. But little Max, on the other paw...

"And Mom, Dad," said Max, "I know the animals in AC City will tolerate me, no problem, because, because...they have to. It's the law, and they'll get beaten up real bad if they don't. And, and, I'm not so little anymore. I'm nearly grown-up."

Mr. and Mrs. Loupin looked down at Max. To their eyes, he looked half the size of Wil. Actually, Max did stand higher than half as tall as his big brother, but the begging plea in his eyes made him seem even younger than he was.

The phone rang and Mr. Loupin went into the kitchen to answer it. When he returned he said, "That was Mr. L. Lobo. He's going to take his customized car on the steamboat, and he's taking Theena with him."

Mr. and Mrs. Loupin looked at each other, and then Mr. Loupin said, "Max, we are going to have to think about it. Why don't we all get a good night's rest and see how we feel in the morning?"

Wil gave his brother a nudge of support, and suddenly all of Max's worries vanished.

Edgar got permission without having to plead a word. When his father, Mr. HG, learned that Harold was planning to take his racing car on the steamboat, he immediately declared that he, too, would board the steamship, voyage to AC City, and watch his son race to victory, and Edgar should also be there.

NicNac didn't really make a sales pitch. He just told his parents who was going and why, and then begged, "Can I go, Dad? Can I? Can I?"

His father replied, "To AC City? That's where your Uncle Fang lives. He owes me money. Maybe if you show up on his doorstep, looking poor and all, he'll get around to paying me back. And, what the hey, with your friends going, it should be a real good thing for you — one of those learning experiences. I'm sure glad you picked such smart friends, NicNac."

$\mathcal{A}$ couple of days later, all of the Hound's Glenn citizens bound for AC City stood on the dock at River Otter City. But there was no *Iffy Queen* there to meet them. For hours they walked around and waited and looked upriver, hoping to see the steamboat rounding the bend. Finally, late in the afternoon, the *Iffy Queen* steamed slowly toward the dock. Deck otters secured the boat's lines to the dock and then extended the gangplank.

The Iffy Queen *steams toward the dock at River Otter City.*

34

From the darkness of the main-deck hold, emerged Pegleg. He noticed Theena, Max, and Harold in the waiting crowd and waved a tired paw at them. A minute later Captain Blighwater came down the stairs from the pilothouse and stepped ashore. He locked his arms behind his back and rocked on his large webbed feet.

"You are the party from Hound's Glenn, I take it," he said.

They nodded their heads.

"Dreadfully sorry to be so late," he said. "But there was...an incident that caused us to proceed slowly. To be precise, for some unknown reason one of the steam pipes to the larboard piston started to leak. *Larboard* means *port*, and port means the left side of the boat — that is, the side that's on your left if you're standing on deck looking forward. Anyway, we tried to fix the pipe as best we could, but still we had to reduce pressure and speed, and so there you have it. But I assure you, we will make every effort to make up the lost time."

"Captain Blighwater," said Mr. L. Lobo, "perhaps we can help you fix that leak. We're pretty good at fixing cars." He nodded toward Wil and Harold.

"Me too," said Theena.

The captain looked down at her. "Ah, yes. My little steam engine expert. Well then, it looks like we shall be full-steam-ahead in no time. Come aboard, all of you."

The grown-ups started by unhooking Harold's car from Numero Uno. They rolled the lowrider over two thick gangplanks onto the *Iffy Queen* and into the cargo hold. Next they did the same with Harold's car.

Meanwhile, an otter steward showed Mr. HG to his cabin, and Theena to the cabin where she and her father were to stay. To save money, Wil, Harold, Max, and NicNac didn't have cabins. They would camp out in sleeping bags in the hold next to the cars.

When the two cars had been secured in the hold — tied down so they couldn't roll back and forth — the otters cast off the dock lines. Up in the pilothouse, Captain Blighwater sounded the steam whistle and steered the Iffy Queen to the middle of the river channel. By then, the sun was close to setting. From the top deck behind the pilothouse, the four young ones looked back at River Otter City. The sunset colors reflected on the stillness of the water. It was growing dark, but even so, Max saw something up the river.

"Hey, is that a little rowboat following us?" he asked the others.

"Oh, yeah. I see it." said Edgar.

Theena and NicNac also saw it, but before they could say so, there was a "swoosh" in the air behind them. They all turned just as a Golden Eagle landed on the pilothouse. Five more circled overhead.

"Captain Machina!" all four canines shouted out to Captain D. X. Machina, the wise and powerful eagle who had resolved the invasion of the birds in Hound's Glenn the previous spring.

"Hello, young ones," said the Golden Eagle, as the circling eagles landed on the top deck. "Are you taking a river cruise with us?"

"We sure are," said Max. "We're going to AC City, to the auto show and car races. Are you taking a river cruise, too?"

"No. It's official business for my squadron and me."

"Is it to protect the secret cargo?" asked Max.

"I can't comment on that," Captain Machina replied, looking a little irritated. "I guess I need to tell Captain Blighwater, 'He who would keep a secret, needs to keep it a secret that he has a secret to keep.' "

Puzzled expressions twisted the muzzles of the four young canines. But NicNac's muzzle seemed especially twisted. He mumbled to himself, "He who

Captain Machina and his squadron arrive at the Iffy Queen.

keep — no, it's he who...who he would...Who's *he*, anyway?"

"Captain Machina," said Max to the eagle, "it looks like someone in a rowboat is following us."

"Yes," replied the captain. "We've been keeping our eyes on him. That's Casanova Cugat, the puma river pirate."

"Pirate!?!" shouted out all four, just a little bit scared.

"Yes, the worst pirate in the history of this river. But we have him under close watch."

The young ones' eyes searched the dark water of the river behind them. But the last rays of the sun didn't reveal the lone puma in the little boat. Not being able to see the pirate just made him seem a little more frightening.

A small bell sounded, and Captain Machina said to the four friends, "That's the dinner bell. You should go below and get something to eat. Don't worry about a thing — we're on watch tonight."

As they walked down the stairs to the second deck, NicNac was still mumbling to himself, "He who would who he keep...would he..."

"It's 'He who would keep a secret,'" said Edgar. "And in this case, it's Captain Blighwater who had a secret to keep."

"And he shouldn't have told us he had a secret to keep," added Theena.

"But he got lucky when it was us he told he had a secret to keep," said Max, "because we aren't going to tell anyone."

"About what?" asked NicNac.

"About Captain Blighwater's secret," said Max.

"What secret?" asked NicNac.

"Good answer," said Edgar.

Chapter Four

A Mysterious Disappearance

Captain Blighwater stood at the entrance to the dining hall, or saloon. He didn't exactly smile when the four young ones approached, but he did seem pleased when he said, "Ah, are you in for a treat tonight! We have after-dinner entertainment. Just like the grandest floating palace on the river, the old *Iffy Queen* will resound with music and laughter."

As it turned out, dinner on the *Iffy Queen* was much less formal than on a floating palace. For one thing, the passengers ate with the off-duty crew at long tables. No waiters served them — it was buffet style. Everyone took a tray and chose from a variety of foods, and with so many different critters aboard, the young ones faced a very strange variety indeed. Of course, they picked only canine food. But they nudged each other and made faces when they passed the containers of food for the otters, bears, and toads.

"There's Pop," said Theena to the others. They carried their trays to Mr. L. Lobo's table.

"Wil and Harold are scrubbing the grease out of their fur," said Mr. L. Lobo as he motioned to the young ones to sit down across from him. Next to Mr. L. Lobo sat Mr. HG, and next to him, Pegleg, who looked much happier than when they had seen him that afternoon.

"Your father's been a real help to us," said Pegleg to Theena. "I reckon by mid morning tomorrow the *Iffy Queen* will be moving at full-steam-ahead."

"Will we arrive in time for the start of the car show?" asked Theena.

"Sure as to that," said Pegleg. "And because we aren't picking up any cargo along the way, we may even be a day or so early."

A few minutes later, Wil and Harold came to the table with their trays piled high with canine food. They both looked tired but content.

"Well, Harold, think you'll be ready for the race?" asked Mr. HG.

"Zero doubt about that, Dad," said Harold. "Wil and I are on it."

"You know, Pegleg," said Mr. L. Lobo, "That hole in the larboard piston pipe looked like it had been done kind of deliberate-like."

"Aye, you're in the right as to that," said Pegleg. "Very suspicious it be. But we've got the captain looking into it, so mum's the word."

"Captain Blighwater is looking into it?" asked NicNac. "The one who has a secret to keep?"

"Not Captain Blighwater," replied Pegleg. "Captain Machina."

"Captain Machina is he who would keep a what, would he be?" asked NicNac.

"Mum's the word," suggested Edgar without looking up from his plate.

"Who what who would who..." sputtered Pegleg.

"Us is who," said Max, and the other young ones nodded while their elders looked at one another with puzzled expressions.

When all in their group had finished eating, they took their trays of dirty dishes to the kitchen, which is called a *galley* on a boat. Before returning to the table to settle down for the night's entertainment, all the canines, except the young ones, grabbed a can of Tuffy's Toilet Water. As soon as all the critters in the saloon settled in, Captain Blighwater stepped onto the little stage. The lights dimmed, and only a spotlight lit the captain.

"Tonight, our entertainers have a really big show for you," he announced. "Well, to be perfectly frank, it's about as big as last night's really big show. But tonight, because we have such a full house, with special guests all the way from Hound's Glenn, our entertainers planned some really big numbers. Everyone, please give a warm round of applause to our world-class piano player, Tuxedo Thomas!"

When the Hound's Glenn's canines saw the eight-hundred-pun gorilla come onto the stage — well, they

42

did look a bit worried. But Tuxedo held up his arms and looked at the canines. "Calm your worried minds," he said. "I'm done and finished with joke telling. It might surprise you, but in my early years I trained as a serious musician, and so I can tickle these black and white keys as fine as your ears can stand."

"And may I be frank again...," said the captain, and he started to chuckle, "even though my name is Blighwater..."

"With jokes like that, I may have to go back to joke telling," said Tuxedo. The Hound's Glenn canines were barely able to smile politely at the thought of that.

"The matchless talent of Tuxedo tonight," continued Blighwater, "will be matched by the spectacular and bewitching voices of the best singing trio on this animal's continent. I give you...the Pumettes!"

The trio of female singers stepped onto the stage. Their short fur was the color of golden-hued sand — a desert color for high-dwelling mountain lions, or *pumas* as some called them. One stepped a little forward of the others. "I'm Renée," she said, "and no, you're not seeing double — these two are twin sisters, Sylvie and Céline. And together we are the Pumettes."

Everyone clapped loudly, then quieted as Mr. Tuxedo began playing a sweetly sad melody, and Renée began softly singing about a puma she used to love, but who left her because he fell in love with gold and fast living. By the time she finished, nearly everyone in the

43

dining hall had tears in their eyes — except the young male critters. They really couldn't understand what was the big deal. Sure, females could be good friends, but gold…now there was something *everyone* could appreciate.

Fortunately, the remainder of the Pumettes' music set grew increasingly more cheerful and upbeat. When they finished, the whole saloon stood and stamped their paws on the floor and tables — some of the critters even howled.

"Thank you all. You're a wonderful audience," said Renée. "We're going to take a short break now, and we'll be back in just fifteen minutes."

The Pumettes and Tuxedo Thomas entertain the passengers.

44

Max, Edgar, and NicNac quickly stood up and left the table. Just before they bolted through the door, Max noticed that Theena had remained seated.

"Hey, Theena," he called. "Don't you want to see the furnaces at night?"

"No, you go ahead," she called back. "Maybe later."

The three young canines hurried down to the lower deck and into the engine room, where fires burned hot in the furnaces for the steam boiler. Outside, the evening had cooled down, but inside the engine room the furnaces warmed the stokers and anyone else who came near. The cubs and pup stopped just out of the way of the four bears who were taking turns stoking the furnaces. One of the bears noticed them and took a break from throwing firewood into the furnace. The flickering light from the furnace fires lit the engine room, and that made everything and everyone seem just a bit spooky. But the bear smiled broadly at the little ones.

"Hello. You young canines came down to see how a steamship works at night?" he asked them.

"We sure did," said Max. "Doggies, that looks like hard work!"

"It can be," said the bear. "But the boat is running at quarter speed, so we don't have to keep the furnaces burning too terribly hot."

"Excuse me, Mr. Bear," began Edgar, "but I thought all you bears lived in the mountains and worked in the gold mines."

"Call me Cal," said the bear. "Normally, we do work in the mines. But the four of us thought we'd take a little river cruise — kind of a working vacation. So we arranged to relieve four of the otters, who wanted a holiday in the mountains."

Cal asked them how they liked the river so far, and the young canines said they liked it just fine. Then they went on to tell of the car show and car racing in AC City.

Meanwhile, up on the passenger and dining hall deck above them, Theena had followed Renée out of the saloon, hoping to talk to her. Leaning against the railing and staring into the darkness of the night,

Cal takes a break from stoking a furnace in the engine room.

Renée, who wore a black cloak and hood, seemed to Theena to have an air of deep sadness.

Just as Theena was about to say "Hi," Renée turned her head to the wolf cub and smiled.

"I really liked your singing," said Theena.

"Thanks," said Renée, who turned her muzzle to face the darkness again. Without looking at Theena she asked, "Aren't you worried about getting cold out here?"

"No, not much," replied Theena, but she began to wonder if she was bothering the singer. "Well, I just wanted to tell you how much I liked your singing."

"Wait, don't go," said Renée. "Tell me about yourself. Tell me where you're traveling to."

"We're going to the car show in AC City. My pop is going to win the grand prize for his customized car."

"AC City is a great town," Renée said. "I wish I could go there, but I have other plans — places to be, things to do, critters to be with."

"Is the puma you were singing about one of those critters?" asked Theena.

"It shows, huh?" said Renée.

Theena didn't know what to say to that, so after a few silent seconds, she began telling Renée about her father's auto-body and repair shop and how she liked working in it, and also about her three best friends, Max, Edgar, and NicNac.

"Is any one of those three extra-special to you?" Renée asked.

Theena talks to Renée on deck during the Pumettes' break.

Theena, about to answer, stopped when Renée suddenly looked away, at two shadowy figures approaching out of the darkness.

"Excuse me, Theena," said Renée. "It's the sisters." She moved toward the other two pumas, also covered in floor-length, black hooded cloaks.

Theena heard the Pumettes whispering to one another as she re-entered the dining hall. And she thought she heard one of the sisters say the words "tidy sum."

Of the young ones, only Theena and Edgar had beds in their fathers' cabins. Max and NicNac slept in sleeping bags in the cargo hold, and so did Wil and Harold. It had been a long day, and so even though the

48

deck was hard and the noise from the steam pistons loud, they all quickly fell asleep.

In the morning, they woke and stretched in their sleeping bags, and then climbed out, stood, and stretched some more. When they reached the dining hall, they didn't see the others. But Wil and Harold, knowing they had a full day's work ahead of them, didn't want to wait to eat. They all grabbed trays and were soon wolfing down big bowls of canine breakfast food. As they finished their meals, Mr. L. Lobo and Theena and then Mr. HG and Edgar joined them.

"So, Mr. L. Lobo, do you think you'll have that steam engine fixed in no time?" asked Mr. HG.

"In no time at all," answered Mr. L. Lobo. "In a couple of hours the boat is going to stop to refuel. We'll be able to shut down the larboard engine and replace that leaky steampipe."

Mr. HG turned to his son and Wil and said, "Looks like you two will have to take a break from your mechanical endeavors to load firewood."

"Load firewood, Dad?" asked Harold. "But we have to keep working on the engine rebuild."

"Well, maybe the young ones can take your places loading wood," said Mr. HG.

"Us?" said Edgar.

"It's the tradition," said Mr. L. Lobo. "Nobody rides for free on a riverboat, and cargo-hold passengers always pay by loading firewood."

"That's okay with me, Pop. I don't mind," said Theena.

"No. You're going help me on the repairs," said Mr. L. Lobo. "You're the expert on steam engines."

Just then Captain Blighwater walked into the dining hall, wringing his hands and looking around as if searching for someone in particular. He climbed onto the stage and held up his hands.

"Ahem. Terribly sorry to interrupt your morning meal, but has anyone seen Tuxedo this morning, or even late last night? Anyone?...at all?...Well, if you do know something about his...about where he might be, or whether he was carrying a tidy...er...package, please tell Captain Machina or myself."

The Golden Eagle, who had been listening from the back of the room, came on stage.

"Might as well tell you all straight out — Tuxedo Thomas is missing," Captain Machina announced. "I suppose he could have fallen overboard sometime after he and the Pumettes finished their last set. But how he could have fallen overboard without us hearing a splash or a yell for help, I simply don't know. It's almost as if he had decided to go for a midnight swim, never to return."

Chapter Five

The Worst Pirate Ever

*T*uxedo had indeed gone for a midnight swim, but it wasn't exactly his decision. The hypnotic eyes of a female puma had encouraged him to quietly lower himself into the water and swim away from the riverboat. When he awakened from the hypnotic spell, he found himself in the middle of a night-dark river, so far away from the boat he couldn't even hear it. He stopped swimming and let himself just float upon the water. He felt awfully alone in the darkness.

It occurred to him he should swim to the nearest riverbank, but just as he started, he heard the splash of oars. Upstream and from out of the darkness, a rowboat glided straight at him. It almost hit him in the head, but he ducked aside, and then, holding onto his hat, he also ducked the oar blade. Before the boat passed him on by, he reached up and grabbed the stern, pulled himself up a little, and looked right into the eyes of a puma.

The puma looked back at the gorilla head in complete disbelief.

"Don't just sit there, old sport," said Tuxedo. "Give us a hand, like a good chap."

"There's n-n-no room for you," sputtered the puma.

"I'm afraid I must insist," said Tuxedo as he climbed aboard. They sat in silence for a minute. The puma wondered if he had fallen asleep and was now dreaming about a large gorilla in a top hat sitting across from him. Tuxedo wondered about the hypnotic Céline and whether she was related to this rowboat puma.

"Would you be so kind as to row me ashore, Mr.... ?" asked Tuxedo.

"...Smith," said the puma. "Casanova Smith."

"Ah, yes. Mr. Smith. Of course it is," said the gorilla. "Enchanted to meet you — even in these unusual circumstances. My name is Tuxedo Thomas. I'm an entertainer who seems to have fallen off his place of employment, namely the *Iffy Queen*. I simply have to get back aboard — the show must go on, you know."

"I have to catch up with that riverboat," said Casanova. "I have...My twin sisters and my ex-girlfriend are aboard that boat, and I have important news to tell them. So I can't row you ashore."

"Ah, well," said Tuxedo. "Seeing as how you are the captain of this fine vessel, I bow to your wishes. Do allow me, however, to assist you with the rowing. You secure those oars and move yourself onto the front seat."

Casanova, exhausted from rowing all day and half the night, nodded in agreement, and wearily moved to the bow of the rowboat. Without rocking the boat even a little, Tuxedo deftly moved himself into the boat's middle seat, facing the stern in rowing position.

"You know, on second thought," said Tuxedo, "it might be better if you sat facing me — for the sake of pleasant conversation."

He reached one arm behind himself, seized Casanova by the throat, lifted him off the bow seat, and gently placed him in the stern seat.

"Please excuse me for being so forward," Tuxedo said as he took the oars in hand. "I didn't hurt you, did I?"

Casanova tried to gasp out "No," but he could only clutch at his throat.

"Good," said Tuxedo. "Well, it's full-speed-ahead, then."

For the remainder of the night, the gorilla rowed the boat at a good pace while the puma slept. Just at sunrise Tuxedo looked ahead, hoping to catch sight of the *Iffy Queen* or even its wake. Unfortunately, he saw nothing but dark, glassy smoothness. But around the next bend in the river, he noticed several buildings on the bank. *It looks like Buccaneer Landing,* he thought.

He gently kicked at the sleeping puma. Casanova opened his eyes and stretched as all cats like to do when they awake. Then he froze. He stared in wide-eyed surprise at the gorilla rowing his boat. After a few seconds, the odd events of last night returned to his memory.

"Any sign of the *Iffy Queen*?" Casanova asked. He went back to stretching.

"Nary a one," said Tuxedo. "Wouldn't you like me to row us ashore to that little town over there?"

"No! The riverboat might be just around the next bend. They have to stop to refuel sooner or later."

"You certainly are correct in thinking that," said Tuxedo. "However, I do remember the captain mentioning that the engines would be fully repaired at the next stop. Once they do that...well, you will have

Just as the sun rises, Tuxedo Thomas nudges Casanova Cugat with his foot, and the puma awakes, wide-eyed with surprise.

no chance of catching up with a steamboat moving full-steam-ahead."

"Hmm," purred the puma. "What we need is a faster boat. Row us over to that dock and I'll see what I can find."

"Have you the money to purchase such a boat?" asked Tuxedo as he aimed the boat toward the dock.

"I have my ways. I can be very convincing. Look into my eyes," said the puma.

Ah, yes, Tuxedo thought to himself. *"Look into my eyes." That's the last thing I remember Céline telling me. I'd better not…* But then he decided to take a chance and play along.

So Tuxedo stared back at the puma's golden eyes. To his surprise, he felt nothing. That is to say, he didn't feel like he was being hypnotized at all. But because he had a secret plan, he pretended he was in a trance.

"You will let me do all the talking," said Casanova Cugat. You will not try to contact anyone or run away."

"Yes, Master," said Tuxedo, who felt a little bit silly saying those words, but Casanova didn't seem to be suspicious.

"You will forget everything I say until I tell you to wake up," said Casanova.

"Yes, Master," said Tuxedo.

"'Yes, Master,'" repeated Casanova. "I like that. Wait till I tell that sister of mine. Céline thought I'd lost my touch — all because I couldn't keep Renée under my spell. What do you think of that, you big dumb gorilla?

I, Casanova Cugat, the greatest river pirate who ever lived — lost my touch? Who're they kidding? I'm still the greatest. And I'd be gold-bar rich right now if Céline hadn't messed up my brilliant plan. She was supposed to damage those engines enough so I could catch up with that rivertub. But she failed — miserably! So what if she can hypnotize critters!

"Say, that gives me a terrific idea. She can hypnotize the bears and the eagles and anyone else who gets in our way. Why didn't I think of it before? Probably because my brain contains so many brilliant plans that it has a hard time choosing which one to think up next! You don't have that problem, do you, you big dumb ape?"

He would have gone on praising himself for the rest of the morning, but a shout from the dock interrupted his bout of self-love.

"Ahoy there, in the row boat — you fixin' to tie up here?" asked an old river otter. "Throw me your lines and I'll secure your boat."

Tuxedo (acting as best he could like someone under a spell) stopped rowing and threw the otter a line. With the boat secured, the gorilla and puma climbed onto the dock and stood in front of the old otter.

"We need a fast boat," said Casanova.

"And what's the reason being for that?" asked the otter.

"Never you mind my reasons, old-timer," said Casanova. "Have you got such a boat?"

"To be sure, my little sailboat is the fastest sailing boat on the river," said the otter. "But what you need to do is wait for the next riverboat to come along."

"Waiting isn't what I do," said Casanova. "Show me the boat."

"Always proud to show off my sailboat — she's just over there," said the otter. Casanova rushed over to inspect the boat. The otter was about to follow him, but Tuxedo put his hand on the otter's shoulder and held him back. The gorilla put a finger to his lips and then started to whisper in the otter's ear. Just before Casanova returned, Tuxedo whispered, "The bears will pay you for the boat on their way back up the river, and so when he tells you to look into his eyes, remember to act like you're hypnotized."

"It's got a little outboard engine," said Casanova. "It's perfect. Now let's talk price, shall we?"

"I use it for festival days here at Buccaneer Landing," said the otter. "It's not for sale."

"Oh, I don't know about that. I can be very convincing," said Casanova as he began to stare into the otter's eyes. "Look into my eyes."

The old river otter stared back at the puma. Then, with a jerk of his head, he opened his eyes wide, and his eyeballs began to roll in circles.

Perfect, thought Tuxedo.

"How about a trade?" purred the puma. "My boat for yours. Sound like a deal, old-timer?"

"Yes, Master," said the old otter.

"Great," said Casanova. "A pleasure doing business with you. So long, chumps."

"Wait, Master," said Tuxedo. "Take me with you. I can help you work the boat."

"Hmm, maybe I could use a big dumb ape like you. Alright, hurry up. Let's cast off."

Tuxedo followed Casanova over to the boat, and before he climbed aboard he paused to read aloud the name on the stern, "*Buccaneer.*"

"What's that you said?" asked the puma.

"*Buccaneer*," said Tuxedo. "The name of the boat — it's another name for a pirate."

But the puma didn't seem to hear him. He was too busy trying to start the little engine. It took a few hard pulls of the starting rope to make it roar to life. Tuxedo cast off the lines and they sped away. Tuxedo was glad Casanova's focus kept him looking down the river, not back at the dock, where the old river otter held his stomach and laughed and laughed.

In a few minutes the *Buccaneer*, the fastest sailboat on the river, motored around a bend in the morning calm. The wake of the boat stretched behind them like a giant "V," causing waves that lapped at the river banks — that is, until the outboard motor sputtered to a stop. In the silence, the two animals looked at each other. Suddenly, Casanova let out a screech that in the old days would have sent shivers down the spine of the big cat's prey.

Tuxedo fought back an impulse to laugh. *This has to be the absolutely worst pirate in the history of the Iffy River,* he thought to himself.

"We're out of gas!" shouted Casanova.

"So it would appear," said Tuxedo.

"What terrible rotten luck for such a fantastic feline as me," said Casanova. "Now we'll have to row again."

"Perhaps not, Master," said Tuxedo. "I've inspected the sails, and we have a rather large downwind sail that we can put up. And the developing wind appears to be blowing our way — that is, down the river."

Under Tuxedo's direction, they hoisted the large downwind sail, which is called a *spinnaker.* At first

The breeze fills the spinnaker of the Buccaneer.

59

the sail fluttered a bit in the breeze, but then with a snap it filled with wind and became as round as a hot-air balloon. The motion of the boat sailing quickly downriver made Casanova smile with satisfaction. But his expression turned sour as he looked up and saw a pirate's skull and crossbones emblazoned on the sail, announcing to the world that a pirate was coming.

Chapter Six

The Plots Thicken

$\mathcal{M}$eanwhile, back on the *Iffy Queen*, the four young ones relaxed on the upper deck. They had a couple of hours before the steamboat was to stop and they would load firewood (except Theena, who was to help her father with the steam engine repair).

"I think it's really suspicious that Tuxedo disappeared last night," said Max. "And I think it has something to do with Captain Blighwater's secret."

"Me too," said NicNac, and then after a moment, "What secret?"

"It's not much of a secret anyway," said Max. He told Theena and me about it the first day we met him. It's about his tidy sum of money."

Theena nodded "yes" in agreement, but said nothing. She looked a bit sad and a bit worried.

"Do you think Tuxedo stole the money?" asked NicNac.

"I don't know," said Max. "It's kind of hard to believe he did."

"It could be that Tuxedo was guarding the money for the captain," suggested Edgar, "and the critter that stole the money also made Tuxedo disappear."

"That would mean the thief is still aboard," said Max, "since Tuxedo seems to be the only one who's missing."

"How come Captain Machina didn't go looking for Mr. Gorilla?" asked NicNac. "He should have. Tuxedo might be in trouble."

"Perhaps Captain Machina has to stay with the boat," said Edgar. "Perhaps the *real* secret is still *on the boat*. I've been thinking. Bears usually work in the gold mines in Minersville. Captain Blighwater said he had an important cargo to pick up in Minersville. And that's where the bears got onboard. Perhaps... "

"There's a shipment of gold on this boat!" shouted Max.

Gold!

Alarmed, his friends shushed him. Max felt embarrassed. He looked around to see if anyone had heard him, but there was no one nearby.

"That's probably the real secret alright," said Edgar. "But who's planning to steal the gold?"

"Well, we know that Casanova Cugat is a pirate," Max began slowly. "And we know that he is a puma, and we know that the Pumettes are pumas, and so... "

"Stop it!" shouted Theena. "That's not fair! Renée is a nice animal. She can't be a thief."

Theena jumped up, and her friends watched as she disappeared down the stairs. But none of them noticed that Captain Machina, perched on top of the pilothouse, had been staring at them with his eagle eyes. He was about to say something to the young ones, but before he could, the *Iffy Queen*'s steam whistle shrieked. The riverboat was just about to dock at Beaver Landing.

With the steam whistle sounding again and again, the three remaining young ones ran right past the Golden Eagle and down to the lower deck to help with the loading of firewood.

*A*n hour-and-a-half later, the firewood had been loaded onboard, the beavers had been paid with an IOU from Captain Blighwater (because he no longer had his tidy sum of money), and most important, the steam engines were fixed. The river otters began to cast off the dock lines. The captain and crew had the *Iffy Queen* ready to race down the Iffy River all the way to AC City. But before all the dock lines were

untied, some of the river otters shouted and pointed at something up the river, and everyone looked in that direction. Just coming around the river bend was a small sailboat with a large balloonlike sail, and on that sail they could plainly see the skull-and-crossbones.

"Pirates!" shouted the young ones.

But as the boat sailed past them, they could see a gorilla in a top hat steering it.

"It's Tuxedo!" shouted NicNac.

"Help!" shouted Tuxedo. "I can't stop this crazy thing!"

What the critters on the *Iffy Queen* couldn't see was Casanova, hiding under some sail bags and telling Tuxedo what to say. As the little sailboat sailed down the river and started around the next bend, everyone waved good-bye to Tuxedo. The river otters cast off the last of the dock lines. Captain Blighwater pulled the whistle cord, and the steam whistle shrieked again, letting everyone know that it was full-steam-ahead. The *Iffy Queen* began to speed up, moving twice as fast as she had before the repairs. She quickly rounded the bend and then slowed to a near stop. Ahead of them — in the water, not in the boat — floated Tuxedo.

The sailboat was nowhere in sight. Everyone's eyes focused on the gorilla waving his top hat. A river otter threw him a lifeline. After Tuxedo climbed aboard, the animals gathered around him, each of them very curious as to why he had disappeared. Tuxedo didn't stop to explain. Instead he walked, as if in a trance, up the stairs to his cabin, where he just sat in the dark.

The four young ones followed him, but when they saw the two captains approach, they hid themselves next door, in Theena's father's cabin. From there they listened through the wall as the gorilla told his story to Captain Blighwater and Captain Machina.

When Tuxedo described how Céline had hypnotized him and sent him for a midnight swim, Theena exclaimed, "It was *Céline* — not Renée!"

The other young ones shushed her, and they all listened, fascinated, as Tuxedo continued with his story. They had to hold their muzzles shut to keep from laughing out loud when Tuxedo described just how conceited Casanova was, and what a dumb pirate he turned out to be. Then they learned something very important about how justice is done in the animal kingdom.

"I say we arrest all the Pumettes right this very minute," said Captain Blighwater.

You can't do that, thought Theena. *Renée didn't steal anything.*

"We can't do that," said Captain Machina. "You know the rules. We have to catch them in the act, or with the stolen goods on them. Anyway, as far as we know right now, it's only Céline, and she's too smart to have the tidy sum on her. She probably hid it after she sent Tuxedo on his way, and this boat is too big for us to secretly search everywhere. We'll wait until someone makes a move."

"Casanova wanted me to give the twins a message," said Tuxedo. "It's rather long, to say the least."

"Wait a minute," said Captain Machina. "Just the twins? Not Renée?"

"Just the twins," said Tuxedo. "He said to tell them that the big dumb ape — meaning me — is hypnotized, and who's the greatest hypnotizer now? He goes on in that vein at some length. Eventually, he related to me the nub of the message. He wants the twins to hypnotize the bears and you and your eagle squadron..."

"Har-rumph," said Captain Machina. "And just how is Céline supposed to hypnotize so many animals at the same time? Sounds like horse feathers to me. Anyway, an eagle can outstare any animal on this continent."

"I know, I know," answered Tuxedo. "The depth of this puma's ignorance is beyond belief. This *is* Casanova's big scheme, though, if I may continue... The twins are then to steal the gold, and after dark Casanova, after he refuels the *Buccaneer*, will bring it alongside. They are to drop the box of gold bars into the boat. He will then speed away — without his sisters, hide in the swamp, and meet up with them sometime in the future."

"Alright," said Captain Machina. "Here's what we'll do. You go on pretending you're still hypnotized, and you give the twins the message. When they make their move, we'll catch them in the act."

"What about my money?" asked Captain Blighwater.

"Your tidy sum of money?" said Captain Machina. "Don't worry. When we catch them in the act of stealing the gold, we can search their cabin, and maybe we'll find your tidy sum and Céline will confess to stealing it, as well as admitting she made that hole in the larboard piston pipe."

"Maybe?" said the toad in a hoarse croak.

The two captains left Tuxedo sitting in the dim cabin and quietly shut the cabin door behind them. Then Captain Blighwater bellowed out, "Attention, all crew members! Attention, all passengers!"

At the sound of his very loud voice, most all of the crew and passengers turned their heads in his direction. Even the Pumettes, who had a cabin on the other side of the boat, could hear him.

"Tuxedo appears to be in a deep hypnotic trance," the captain shouted, "and we don't know how to wake him. We, for certain, don't know how he came to be in this condition. Not the foggiest notion of why or how. We suspect no one! We intend to leave him alone — completely unguarded — and wait and hope for something or other to happen."

Inside his cabin, Tuxedo sighed. Outside the cabin, Captain Machina sighed. Inside Theena's father's cabin, the four young ones sighed, rolled their eyes, and shook their little muzzles from side to side. And they all thought the same thing: *The captain of the* Iffy Queen *is a good old river toad, but is he ever a terribly bad, bad actor!* They all felt certain that Céline would be suspicious now, and it would be near impossible to catch her in the act of stealing the gold.

Céline herself was thinking that the captain had given a strange, if not a suspiciously loud, speech. For the rest of the afternoon, she and Sylvie talked about it and kept telling each other that it would be dangerously dumb to go talk to Tuxedo after a speech like that. Still, the trance she had used on Tuxedo would surely have worn off by now. And the idea that her brother might have encountered Tuxedo and actually hypnotized him really ate at Céline. She had to know for certain. So as the glow of sunset turned into twilight, and while most everyone else sat in the saloon eating dinner, she and Sylvie put on their cloaks and, as silent as cats, crept over to Tuxedo's cabin. Pumas excel at creeping about, just like in the old days when they hunted down their dinner.

But canines, too, are pretty good at hunting and tracking. The four young ones had decided to keep an eye on the Pumettes' cabin, and NicNac had volunteered for the first turn of watching. When he spied the twin sisters leaving their cabin and heading for Tuxedo's, he waited until they turned a corner, and then he raced into the saloon.

"I have a secret that I would keep," he whispered to his three friends sitting at the table. They jumped up and followed him out of the saloon and to Theena's father's cabin. Quietly they all crept into the cabin and pressed their ears to the wall.

They could hear Céline's voice saying, "You look as though you've finally recovered from your ordeal."

A couple of seconds passed before they heard Tuxedo answer, "Yes, it was quite an ordeal at that. Unfortunately, I remember very little of it. Very odd, that."

"I think you must have spent some time with our brother," said Céline.

"Your brother?" asked Tuxedo, who was pretty good at acting, unlike a certain toad we're too polite to name.

"Yes, our brother," said Céline. "We know he was following us in a small boat. He must have saved you after you fell overboard, and then put you in a trance — which has already worn off, since he's not very good at trances. Perhaps I can help you recall some of what happened to you.

"Our brother looks just like us, you know," Céline continued, "especially around the eyes. Look at my eyes. See how much they look like his. Look deeply…"

"Is he under again?" asked Sylvie. "Ask him if Casanova gave him a message."

"Did the puma who rescued you give you a message for us?" asked Céline.

Céline hypnotizes Tuxedo once again.

For the second time the young ones heard Casanova's message for the twins. When Tuxedo finished, there was a moment of silence, and then Céline exclaimed, "That's it?! That's Casanova's grand plan? What a doofus! How does he expect me to hypnotize four bears, a squadron of eagles, and anyone else who happens to be standing around? All at the same time? Forget that, and forget him!"

"What'll we do?" asked Sylvie.

"It's a good thing we stole the toad's money," said Céline. "Let's just take that and skedaddle out of here."

"I'm with you," said Sylvie. "But how? The minute they see us trying to leave the ship, they're sure to ask us about the money."

"Hmm, I might know a way…," said Céline. "Sandbar Point should be just ahead…"

The next thing the young ones heard was the quiet closing of Tuxedo's cabin door. They waited a few seconds, and then Max cracked open their door to peer outside.

"They're gone," said Max. "Let's go see if Tuxedo's okay."

He wasn't. His half-opened eyes stared blankly ahead and he didn't seem to recognize the young ones.

"Do you think if we yell loud enough he'll wake up?" asked Max.

"It might not be funny to suddenly wake an eight-hundred-pun gorilla," suggested Edgar.

"Here, I'll splash a little water on his cheeks," said Theena. She poured a glass of water from the vanity sink faucet. Carefully she applied little drips and drabs of water to his face. But the blank-faced gorilla didn't respond.

"Let me help," said NicNac as he took the water glass from Theena's hand and threw the entire glassful in Tuxedo's face. The gorilla's eyes became as big as white saucers and his mouth opened wide, showing his gleaming white teeth. Frightened by this, the young ones quickly backed away, pressing themselves against the wall.

71

"Wow. Was that ever a wake-up," said Tuxedo. He shook his head and then smiled at the four. "Thanks. Did you happen to hear what happened while Céline had me hypnotized?"

"We sure did," said Max. The four took turns explaining that Tuxedo had given Céline and Sylvie the message from Casanova Cugat. And they told him what Céline had said about it. In the end, they weren't sure what the twins would do next, but they all agreed that Casanova had to be just about the worst pirate in the history of the Iffy River.

Chapter Seven

Ups and Downs

*C*asanova Cugat hadn't a clue as to how badly his gold-stealing scheme was falling apart. After ordering Tuxedo to jump into the water and wait for the *Iffy Queen* to come around the bend, Casanova had continued sailing down the river. Soon he came to a little river port — so little that it was more like a small dock on an empty riverbank. He beached the sailboat, lowered the sails, to hide the skull-and-crossbones, and watched as the *Iffy Queen* steamed on by.

After it disappeared around the next bend, he tried to hypnotize the local boat owners into giving him a tank of gas. They just laughed at him and told him to knock it off. In the end, he had to trade — for just one tank of gas — the mast of the sailboat, all the sails, and an ivory peg leg better than the one he had lost to Pegleg years ago (Casanova had amazing luck in finding peg legs washed up on beaches).

With the outboard engine pushing the little boat at full speed, he soon caught up with the wake of the steamboat, and by that he knew that the *Iffy Queen* wasn't too far ahead. Slowing the engine, he laughed aloud and began dreaming of all the gold that would soon be his.

In the pilothouse the captains listened to Tuxedo tell of the twin sisters' visit. The young ones had tried to follow the gorilla into the pilothouse, but Captain Machina had shut the door in their little faces. Stealthily, they had crept around to the back of the pilothouse and listened from there.

Tuxedo told how Céline, once again, had hypnotized him. He told how the young ones had overheard the conversation, listening through the wall as they were, and had come to his rescue after the twins left.

"So Céline and Sylvie have the tidy sum," said Captain Machina, "and Casanova is on his way to get the gold. The twins might not be planning to help him with his big gold-stealing scheme. Or maybe they *are* planning to help and Céline just said they weren't because she knew the young ones were listening. Where are those sisters now?"

"The Pumettes should be in their cabin preparing for tonight's performance," said Captain Blighwater.

"Quite right," said Tuxedo. "And I should be getting ready also. I'm in desperate need of a fresh cummerbund. No self-respecting gorilla would think himself ready for the evening without a well-ironed cummerbund."

"Just one last matter before you leave, Tuxedo," said Captain Blighwater. "I simply can't bring myself to believe Renée doesn't have a paw in the theft of my tidy sum of money, or in Casanova's plan to steal the gold. Perhaps, while they're on stage, I'll pay the Pumettes' cabin a little visit and search through all their belongings."

Captain Machina and Tuxedo stared at the toad in disbelief. They left the pilothouse in stony silence. Pegleg, who was steering the *Iffy Queen* down the river, sadly shook his head.

"Well," mumbled Captain Blighwater as he also left the pilothouse, "it's *my* tidy sum of money. And I really need it back."

Pegleg remained in the pilothouse — someone had to steer the boat, after all. Behind the pilothouse, in the darkness of the night, the four young ones whispered so Pegleg wouldn't hear them.

"The nerve of Captain Blighwater, wanting to search an innocent animal's room," said Theena.

"What should we do?" asked Max.

"Go eat dinner and watch the show?" suggested Edgar.

"I'm going to watch the Pumettes' cabin door," said Theena. "You know, just to make sure they go from their cabin straight to the saloon."

Max and Edgar glanced at one another, not quite believing that was all Theena intended to do.

75

"Good idea," said NicNac. "I'll go spy on the gorilla."

The others stared at him. "Why in the world… "
said Edgar.

"I want to see what a cummerbund is," NicNac said.

"Great. We've got a plan — kind of," said Max. "Let's
all meet up in the saloon for dinner."

Soon twilight turned to darkness, made even darker by
a thick fog. Theena waited until the Pumettes left their
cabin. Then she came up behind them.

"Miss Renée?" she called out.

Renée stopped, turned around, and smiled at the
young wolf. "Hello, Theena. You're coming to see us, of
course."

"Yes, I am," said Theena. "But I wanted to ask you
a question about becoming a singer. Do you have a
minute?"

"They won't start the show without me," Renée
smiled "Tell me what you want to know."

Theena waited until the twins entered the saloon,
and even then she felt it better to whisper. "Captain
Blighwater thinks you three stole his tidy sum of money.
He might even search your cabin while
you're singing. And if he finds the money,
he'll blame all three of you."

"Hmm," said Renée. "Would even a
toad stoop so low? Can you wait here
while I run back to my cabin for a moment?"

In less than a minute she returned, a concerned look on her face. "Do me a favor, little one," she said. "Could you ask your father for a small sack of metal washers?"

Theena was puzzled, but she nodded her head.

"Good," said Renée. "I'd better hurry, or Tuxedo will start telling jokes again."

Theena followed Renée into the saloon, found her father, and whispered in his ear. After a moment of thinking about it, he nodded and whispered back to her. She rushed out, and returned in just a few minutes, carrying a small bag that looked fairly heavy. Finally she sat down to dinner.

When the Pumettes finished their first set of songs, Theena quietly followed Renée out of the saloon. Without saying a word, she walked up beside Renée and held the bag of metal washers just in front of her. Renée reached down as if to put a kind paw on the little one's shoulder, carefully took the bag, and left the saloon, walking toward the Pumettes' cabin.

Just before the second set started, Theena watched Renée return and approach Captain Blighwater. Theena saw the captain smile and then put a finger to the side of his snout and wink. The twins never saw any of this because they hadn't returned from wherever they had gone to. Just as they came back and took their places on stage, Max, Edgar, and

Renée and Captain Blighwater share a secret.

NicNac entered the saloon, loaded their trays at the buffet, and sat down next to Theena.

Max leaned over and whispered to her, "Those twins are up to something. We followed them up to the pilothouse and watched them talking to Pegleg. It looked like Céline was hypnotizing him — but what for? Anyway, we'd better tell the captains."

Just then the riverboat bumped and shook to a stop, and every critter, standing or sitting, fell forward.

"It's Sandbar Point!" wailed Captain Blighwater. "We've run aground! All deck-paws to the main deck!"

The crew of the *Iffy Queen* followed their captain below to the main deck to do whatever was needed to save the boat. The passengers, after picking themselves

up off the floor, milled about in a confused state.
Some were determined to go to their cabins and save
their belongings from who knew what, and some were
curious to see for themselves just what had happened.
The young ones were among the curious who lined the
railing, peering into the gloomy fog and night.

"Are we going to sink?" asked Max.

"How can we sink if we're on the ground?" asked
NicNac.

"Good point," said Edgar.

"Look! I can see the riverbank," said Theena.

In between the dark billows of fog, they could see
the bank alongside the steamboat. It looked almost
close enough to jump to — except they were on the
second deck and high above the land.

"Did we run into the riverbank?" asked Max.

"No," said Mr. HG. "I'm pretty sure we ran into a
sandbar that sticks out from the riverbank."

"Let's go ask the captain if we can help," said
Mr. L. Lobo.

"Good idea," replied Mr. HG. "Harold, Wil, you go
inspect the cars and make sure the tie-downs didn't
break."

"What about the young ones?" asked Wil.

"It would be my pleasure to safeguard my young
friends," said Tuxedo, who had just joined them.

From the railing of the second deck, they watched
as the river otters, each carrying a flashlight, inspected
the hull. Every so often, one would pop his head up

from a hatchway in the lower deck, and yell out, "No leaks in this side of the boat."

Each time the young ones heard that yell, they felt a little bit safer. Their thoughts turned to wondering just how the captain planned to get the boat off the sandbar.

"Tuxedo," asked Theena, as the last otter popped back through the last hatchway, "have you seen Renée?"

"No, and I'm not too sure as to the whereabouts of the twins, either."

"What will we do, Tuxedo?" asked Max. "Are we going to have to get off the boat and walk?"

"Most probably not. I'm fairly certain Captain Blighwater has a plan."

The captain did have a plan. After the crew reported that there weren't any holes letting in water, he made a rather strange request of the passengers.

"Good news, everyone. The *Iffy Queen* is undamaged. However, I want everyone to move to the rear of the boat. I'm going to try to back off the sandbar."

"Why does he want us all in the back of the boat?" asked Edgar.

Just then, as they were walking along toward the stern, they felt the boat move — not forward or backward, but just down a little.

"The boat's become a teeter-totter, balanced on the sandbar," said Max. "When we're all up front, the bow of the boat goes down and the stern goes up."

"And now that we're all at this end of the boat, the back of the boat sinks down and the front rises up," said Theena.

On each of the three decks, passengers and crew gathered themselves at the rear railings and waited. The paddle wheel began to move in reverse — slowly at first, then faster and faster. The water churned white. It sounded like a waterfall. All eyes watched the white water, and all parties hoped for the riverboat to back off the sandbar. But the boat didn't move an inch. When the paddles stopped, all the critters felt a little sad and hopeless.

From the pilothouse, Captain Blighwater called out, "We tried our best, but unfortunately, here we remain — stuck in a spot of bother. I recommend that we all get a good night's sleep, and see what the morning will bring."

Unfortunately for Theena and Edgar, their fathers agreed that, sleepy or not, it was bedtime for the young ones. Max and NicNac, because their sleeping bags were in the hold next to the cars, were able to see and hear everything that happened next. Well, actually, to hear and see everything, they had to sneak out of their bags and hide in the shadows. The first thing they heard was the Golden Eagle's low voice.

"Do you hear that?" Captain Machina asked Tuxedo. After a moment of silence, Max and NicNac could hear the far-away sound of a small engine.

"I do believe an old friend is about to pay us a visit," said Tuxedo.

"Remember, we have to catch him in the act if we want his clan elders to correct his behavior," said Captain Machina.

"How are we going to do that?" asked Captain Blighwater, who had just joined the eagle and the gorilla. "It's obvious that the Pumette twins have deserted us. One of the crew found these two cloaks on the main deck. They must have taken them off so they could wade ashore."

"Yes, they probably have fled the scene," said Tuxedo. "More's the pity for Casanova. He'll be very disappointed when the twins aren't there to hand him the gold, and he might even come to realize that he isn't a very good thief."

"He might, or he might not," said Captain Machina. "It's best if he gets a good scolding from his elders. And for that to happen, we have to catch him stealing. But it would be crime enough for Casanova just to *think* he's stolen the gold. He'd still be guilty."

"In that case, may I suggest a small ruse," said Tuxedo. "Captain Blighwater, let us use those two cloaks. I know two critters they might fit. I shall return forthwith."

In a few minutes Tuxedo returned, along with Wil and Harold, and in the shadows were also Mr. HG, Mr. L. Lobo, and most of the crew. No one wanted to miss the excitement. Of course, there were also two young ones who couldn't sleep, had heard the footsteps of everyone else, and had crept out of their cabins. Theena and Edgar hid in the shadows, close to a railing so they could look down. Theena scanned the passengers at the rails for Renée but didn't see her anywhere.

Wil and Harold put on the twins' cloaks and pulled the hoods over their heads. Tuxedo handed Wil a suitcase loaded with bricks (red bricks, not gold bricks) and gave Harold a powerful flashlight.

Then, while Captain Machina stood guard over the real gold, stowed safely in his cabin, the rest of his squadron dispersed, to keep an eagle eye out for trouble. Tuxedo, Wil, Harold, and Captain Blighwater went down to the main deck, and Tuxedo gave these instructions:

"When Casanova comes alongside, Harold, you turn on the flashlight and point it in his eyes. That way he won't be able to see you. Wil, you place the suitcase in the bow of his boat and then stand back. We'll take it from there."

All of them felt ready, able, and proud to do their duty. Each critter felt supremely confident they would soon capture the worst pirate in the history of the Iffy River.

The outboard engine noise grew louder, and then it stopped as Cugat's boat emerged out of the dark fog and coasted alongside the *Iffy Queen*. Harold switched

on the powerful flashlight. Wil dropped the suitcase
into the bow of the boat, and at the same time, Tuxedo
and Captain Blighwater reached out with boathooks to
seize Casanova.

Unfortunately, the sudden heaviness of the suitcase
in the front of the *Buccaneer* made its bow sink down
and its back rise up. Casanova fell forward, and as
he did, he accidently twisted the outboard motor
throttle. The motor roared. The little boat sped up,
moving forward. The four critters on the main deck of
the *Iffy Queen* all ran forward, trying to keep up with
Casanova's boat, and so did everyone on the upper
decks who had been watching. That made the *Iffy*

Casanova Cugat motors alongside the Iffy Queen, *expecting to pick up a small shipment of gold.*

Queen teeter-totter suddenly forward, and that caused a wave that pushed the *Buccaneer* away from the riverboat. After a second, the *Buccaneer* disappeared into the fog, and the roar of its outboard engine grew steadily less loud.

"Pity, that," said Captain Blighwater. "It would have been ideal to catch him in the act. But we know he's headed for the Delta Swamp — much the sorrow for him. I'll radio my brother to be on the lookout for him. I need to pay my brother a visit anyway — a little matter of a tidy sum of money I owe him. But mum's the word on that."

Chapter Eight

The Boat Freed, the Puma Treed

*I*n the morning at breakfast, Captain Blighwater announced his plan to set off in one of the *Iffy Queen's* lifeboats to visit his brother, Bufo Bufo, who lived on the far edge of Delta Swamp. Along the way he would keep an eye out for Casanova.

If it hadn't been for the thick fog, eagles from the squadron could have helped in the hunt for Casanova. Except, fog or no fog, Captain Machina felt it best to stay on the *Iffy Queen* and guard the gold.

As Captain Blighwater made his announcement, the critters from Hound's Glenn listened and worried. How were they ever going to reach AC City in time for the race and the car show? When would the captain return to get the riverboat off the sandbar?

After breakfast they watched as the crew lowered a lifeboat into the water. Four river otters climbed into the boat, and each took up an oar. Captain Blighwater climbed aboard last and took a place at the bow. He stood to address the remaining crew and passengers on the *Iffy Queen*.

"You've not heard the last of me," he bellowed toward the boat. "I'll be back if I have to row all the way… "

A river otter named Crispy said something to him that the critters on the riverboat couldn't hear, and then the captain said, in a much quieter voice than before, "What do you mean: I should sit down, I'm rocking the boat? See here, who's the captain, anyway? Oh, all right, but you just keep rowing the boat. What do you mean you're taking a coffee break in ten minutes? This is mutiny, Mr. Crispy!"

The lifeboat drew away from the *Iffy Queen* and into the wall of fog, where it became a ghostly image and then slowly vanished from sight. The critters from Hound's Glenn wandered into the cargo hold together and stood by the two cars.

"Do you think the captain will return soon enough to get the *Iffy Queen* off this sandbar and get it to AC City in time?" asked Mr. HG.

"I don't know," said Mr. L. Lobo. "The car show starts tomorrow."

"I'm worried about Renée!" declared Theena. "She might be in danger, especially when Céline finds out that all she's got is a bag of washers."

Theena had told her friends about the swap she and Renée had made, secretly trading a tidy sum of washers for the captain's tidy sum of money, which

Renée had found stashed under Céline's bed the night before and had returned to the captain.

"I'm sure she'll be all right," suggested Wil. "But maybe some of us could go ashore and see if we can find her."

"There's a town nearby, Turkey-Burger Vultureville," said Harold. "We could go there and ask around."

"The Pumettes might have gone there to catch a bus or even steal a car," said Max. "Then they could escape across the desert."

"I could catch up with them easy in my car," said Harold.

Max looked out the cargo doors and across the deck at the riverbank. Followed by his friends, he raced to that side of the boat and looked up.

"Look, we could use the boat's crane to pick up Harold's car and swing it ashore," he shouted. All the canines, including the grown-ups, came out of the hold to see for themselves.

"You know," said Mr. L. Lobo. "I think that might work. You young ones go find Pegleg and we'll ask him if the crane can lift that much weight."

"Sure as to that," said Pegleg when they found him in the pilothouse doing exactly nothing. "The port and larboard cranes together could lift this whole riverboat."

Pegleg had now fully recovered from Céline's hypnotic trance, which had caused him to run the

Iffy Queen aground on the sandbar so the twins could wade ashore. Captain Blighwater had left him in charge, secure in the knowledge that a riverboat that couldn't move couldn't get into much trouble.

Now Pegleg came down to the main deck. As he started giving advice about setting up the crane and pulleys, the Hound's Glenn canines carefully pushed Harold's car out of the cargo hold and near to the edge of the deck.

"We'll build a kind of sling for the car," Pegleg said to two deck otters. "Slide these wood beams underneath, secure them with rope over the top of the car, and leave some slack so we can attach the hoist hook."

After the otters had the car ready to hoist, the bears volunteered to pull the rope on the pulleys. The young ones held their breath as the crane lifted the car into the air and swung it over to the shore. As the bears slowly let out the rope to set the car down on the land, everyone cheered.

"Too bad we can't use the cranes to lift the boat off this sandbar," said Max.

Theena turned to her father. "Pop, are we going to put your car ashore, too?" she asked.

"No way, Lobocita. With miles of worse-than-no-road until you hit Highway One, Numero Uno would never make it. Or if it did, the body and paint would be a mess."

After Mr. HG gave Wil and Harold some money and advice, the two teens grabbed hold of the crane's block and tackle, the bears gave them a push, and they swung ashore and jumped off. They climbed into the car, and Harold started up the engine and made it roar. Then he let it rumble down to an idle, put the car into gear, and slowly and carefully began to drive across the rough land.

The critters from Hound's Glenn watched Harold and Wil take off across the flat land. But even before the two teens disappeared from sight, Max took off toward the pilothouse to find Pegleg. The other young ones followed along.

"How much water is in the front of the boat?" asked Max when they found Pegleg.

"You mean how deep is the water off the bow?" said Pegleg. "There's a way we can find that out. You see that long cord with the weight attached to it?"

The young ones looked to a post where the coil of cord and its lead weight hung from a hook.

"We calls it a lead line. We tosses the lead into the water, and the marks on the line tells us how deep the water is," said Pegleg. "I suppose you be wanting a demonstration."

Pegleg took the lead line and walked to the front of the boat, keeping the coil in one hand and the weight in the other. When he reached the bow, he lowered the lead weight into the water.

"Now, if we were underway — that is, moving along in the river — I'd be tossing the lead way out in front, and the boat would be catching up to it. But seeing as how we're sitting still as a statue, I can just lower the lead into the water. And there — I can feel that it's found the bottom. Now I pull the rope taut — but without pulling the lead up off the bottom, like this. You can see that the "3" mark is just above the water. This old boat only needs about two marks of water, so we know the bow isn't sitting on the bottom."

"Can we try measuring the depth all along the boat?" asked Max. "Maybe we can figure out exactly where the sandbar is."

"No reason why not," said Pegleg. "It'll make you good riverboaters to know that skill."

Theena and Edgar ran off to find pencil and paper. With the sounding lead in hand, Max walked back from the bow of the boat about ten cub-sized steps. He lowered the lead into the water. NicNac lay down on the deck with his head stuck out over the water. He squinted at the line that Max held steady, and then he called out, "It looks like just about three marks."

"We should write that down," suggested Edgar.

"Here, we can write it next to an outline of the boat," said Theena. She had drawn on the notepad an outline of the *Iffy Queen's* hull. It looked pretty much like what a clothes iron would look like if you turned it over and looked at the bottom. Or, to be perfectly clear, Theena's drawing looked kind of like the outline of the burnt area on a white sheet that a hot clothes iron would make if you set it down on that sheet for too long and smoke started to rise from the ironing board. Or…but surely, you get the picture by now.

The young ones walked ten more cub-steps along the side of the boat facing the shore, lowered the lead,

Max, NicNac, Theena, and Edgar measure the depth of the water.

and wrote down the number of marks. They kept at it, taking measurements closer together when they came to the shallow part. When they reached the back of the boat, they walked across the stern and measured the water depth along the other side of the boat also. They took turns lowering the lead, reading the marks, and writing down the numbers. Back at the bow, they sat on the deck and thought about what the measurements were telling them.

"We know exactly where the sandbar is," said Max.

"It must be here," said Theena as she pointed to the handwritten figures of "1½." "It's just a little back of the center of the boat. It's the only place the water isn't deep enough to float the boat."

Edgar penciled in two lines on each side of the boat outline to show where the sandbar must be. On each side of the boat, in between the two lines, he wrote "Sand."

After taking the pencil from Edgar, NicNac wrote in front of the boat outline: "Plenty deep." Everyone smiled and nodded, and he wrote the same thing at the back of the boat.

"The sandbar isn't very big," said Edgar. "I mean it's not wide at all."

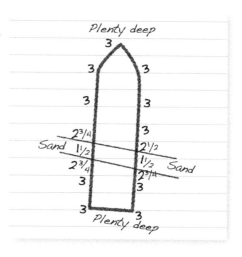

"And more than half of the boat is already past the sandbar," said Theena.

"Too bad we can't pick up the back of the boat and lift it over the sandbar," said NicNac.

"Maybe we can," said Max. "Remember what Pegleg said about the cranes being strong enough to lift the *Iffy Queen*."

"Hold on," protested Edgar. "It can't be done, because the cranes are on the boat. Picture this: A pup wants to raise himself off the ground, so he takes a small crane, ties the rope to his feet, holds the crane in his hands, and starts cranking. What's going to happen?"

"His feet are going to come up in the air?" suggested NicNac.

"Exactly not," said Theena. "The upper part of his body is going to bend down toward his feet."

"Right," said Edgar. "You can't pull yourself up if you have the crane in your hands. And you can't lift the boat if the cranes are on the deck."

"Well, if the crane was down on the ground and then the pup started cranking, I bet he'd get raised up," said NicNac.

"That's it!" said Max. "We can put the cranes on the river bottom."

"Won't they get soggy?" asked NicNac.

"Just the bottoms of the cranes will get wet," said Max. "Most of each crane will be sticking up in the air above the water."

Everyone smiled. They took their diagram and raced up to the pilothouse, where Pegleg had gone just in case any command decisions had to be made.

"What's all the excitement?" Pegleg said as the young ones raced up to him. Max showed him their drawing, and the young ones took turns explaining their plan.

"Hmm, that's a jolly well-thought-out fix-it, that is," said Pegleg. "Let's give her a try. It should be tons more fun than just sitting here watching the river roll by."

For a river otter, *fun* is the key word in any plan. Followed by the young ones, Pegleg descended to the main deck and headed toward the front of the boat. Along the way he told every critter they met to join them at the bow. Even the bears in the engine room and passengers in their cabins were told to assemble up forward.

"Thanks to these little canines, we have a way to get us off this sandbar," Pegleg announced. He explained the plan to everyone, and gave everyone a job to do. The deck otters would detach the port and starboard cranes from the deck. The bears would carefully lower the cranes and wedge them solidly into the river bottom. The otters would attach the hoist hooks that hung down from the two cranes to two iron rings, one on each side of the deck. With everything in place, all hands — half of them on one side of the boat and half on the other side — would grab the ropes that ran from the hoist hooks up through the pulleys and back to the deck, and pull with all their might.

It took most of the rest of the morning to set everything up. Pegleg and the young ones stood on the very front of the bow so they could look along both sides of the boat. The two groups of rope pullers took the slack out of the ropes, and as they pulled hard, they all grunted.

"'Tis music to me ears," said Pegleg, "the sound of other critters working, that is."

Slowly but surely, the back of the *Iffy Queen* did start to rise up. That made the bow dip down in the water a little more, but if anyone noticed it, no one seemed to mind. Everyone, including the Golden Eagles perched on the pilothouse roof, focused on the cranes — some fearing they would break from the strain, others very sure they wouldn't.

"Umm, Pegleg," asked Edgar, "after the back of the boat is lifted up, how do we move forward past the sandbar?"

"Didn't think of that, did you?" said Pegleg. "Well, I did. Maybe, we could've used our engines and paddled forward, but the paddle wheel, as you can see, is almost completely out of the water now. Or we could have set an anchor off the bow and hauled ourselves forward. But that's a lot of work. So in this case, I think we'll just let the river current gently shove us forward."

The river current did move them forward as the boat bottom came free from resting on the sandbar, and the boat began to move downriver.

"We're free!" shouted the young ones as the *Iffy Queen* began to float forward. Everyone cheered.

But as the boat slowly moved downstream, the cranes had to lean forward, which lowered the boat down, and the back end came to rest on the sandbar again. The *Iffy Queen* stopped.

"Not to worry," said Pegleg. "We'll reset the cranes and do it again. It might take two or three tries, but we'll do it yet."

As it turned out, it took only one more try. The bears moved the cranes a little farther aft. After they reset the cranes, rope pullers pulled and grunted. Once again the back part of the boat rose up and the bow went down a little. Slowly the river current nudged them downriver a little more, and this time the *Iffy Queen* didn't stop drifting. They were as free as a leaf floating down a stream.

The bears pulled the cranes back aboard the boat. And soon, with smoke billowing out of the smokestacks and the paddle wheel churning the water white, the *Iffy Queen* moved quickly down the river. Pegleg had gone back to the pilothouse, and now he had a real captain's job to do.

"There's the edge of the Delta Swamp coming into view," said Pegleg.

"Have you notified Captain Blighwater that we're underway?" asked Captain Machina.

"He doesn't have a radio in the lifeboat," said Pegleg, "so I radioed Maison de Bufo Bufo."

"Bless you," said Captain Machina.

"What for?"

"I thought you sneezed."

"No, Maison de Bufo Bufo is the name of the place where Bufo Bufo lives," said Pegleg.

"Bufo Bufo lives at Maison de Bufo Bufo?" asked Captain Machina.

"Yes, except he wasn't there when I radioed. He was out hunting for Casanova Cugat. Captain Blighwater was there, though. And he said to pick him up at the downriver edge of the swamp."

*D*uring the afternoon, the fog burned off, so Captain Machina decided to send out two eagles from the squadron to search for Casanova Cugat and for Captain Blighwater as well. When the *Iffy Queen* reached the downriver edge of the swamp, Pegleg "parked" 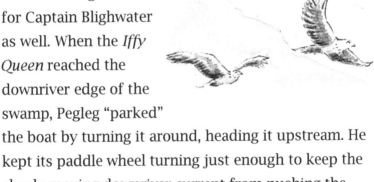 the boat by turning it around, heading it upstream. He kept its paddle wheel turning just enough to keep the slowly moving downriver current from pushing the boat any farther downstream.

"How long can we stay here like this?" asked Max.

"Just as long as we have wood to fire the boilers and make steam," said Pegleg. "And we gots lots of wood." He glanced out the pilothouse window and toward the sky over the swamp. "Well, what do I spy? It's the two eagles. Let's go hear what they have to report."

Pegleg turned over the helm to NicNac (with a helm's-otter to watch over him, of course), and went out onto the deck, followed by Max, Theena, and Edgar. On the upper deck behind the pilothouse, Captain Machina waited for his birds to land, which they did with a swoosh of outspread wings.

"Good news, Captain," said one of the eagles. "It appears that Bufo Bufo and his 'gators have Casanova treed."

"'Gators?" asked Edgar.

"Treed?" asked Max.

"Yes, 'gators. Yes, treed" said the eagle. "After his boat got stuck in the swamp muck, he tried to escape by climbing up a tree. But they have the tree surrounded."

"Send a lifeboat to bring him back," said Captain Machina to Pegleg.

"Aye, but seeing as how the captain took our best rowers, leaving the *Iffy Queen* shorthanded as well, who can I send?" asked Pegleg.

"We'll go," said Max.

"Bravely spoken," said Pegleg, thinking it would be a lot better to have the fathers rowing the boat.

Pegleg got things organized so that when the lifeboat departed, Mr. HG and Mr. L. Lobo were rowing,

with the young ones sitting in the stern. Tuxedo sat
in the bow with a large canvas sack. Remembering all
the rude comments the puma had made about him, he
looked forward to stuffing Casanova into the bag.

The fathers faced backwards on the lifeboat and
couldn't see where they were rowing to. So in the
front of the boat, Tuxedo peered into the deepening
darkness of the junglelike maze of waterways, with
small islands, and dense groves of trees growing in the
shallow water. After they had gone a little way, he said,
"I think our proper course is just a little more over to the
rowers' left."

"Are we a little bit lost?" asked Theena.

"Hopefully not more than just a tad off our intended
course," replied Tuxedo. "But, I must say, this swamp is
a dark, frightful maze, and… Look! Up ahead. Do you
see it? Lanterns!"

Just a little way away, three lanterns shone dimly in
the gloom of dark shadows. The lanterns were moving
toward the lifeboat, and then, out of the darkness
appeared a sight the young ones would never have
imagined: three giant toads, each holding a lantern and
standing on the back of an alligator.

"Good evening, *mes amies*," called out the toad in
the middle. "I am Bufo Bufo. Follow us, if you will. It's
just a little bit farther."

As the critters followed the lantern light, Max had
a question for any of the grown-ups who might know

100

the answer: "Do the alligators mind the toads riding on their backs?"

It was Mr. HG who answered first, "Not at all. You see, after the Great Conversion … "

"That's when animals stopped eating other animals," said Edgar.

"Right — and also it was when all us critters were given speech, and the right to live in houses and drive cars and what-not. Anyway, after the GC some critters said 'thank you very much for the freedom of speech — we'll take it. But as to houses and such, we prefer to live like our ancestors.'"

An alligator cruised up just behind the lifeboat at that point, keeping out of the way of the oars, but close enough to speak to the little canines.

Casanova Cugat is surrounded by toads riding on alligators.

"It really is a wonderful feeling, gliding along in the water, you know," he said. "And the way we're built... well, driving cars and living in houses wouldn't really suit us. The toads take care of all that land-based stuff. They keep us supplied with tofu dinners and crunchy snacks, and we give them rides. It works out quite neatly."

Farther up ahead, they could hear alligator voices and see more lantern lights. Several alligators were surrounding a tree that stuck up out of the shallow water.

"Oh, please come down," said one 'gator. "We promise not to eat you."

"Perish the thought," said another. "We just want to hold you in our jaws."

"Yes, our snaggly, sharp-toothed jaws," said a third.

Directed by Tuxedo, the rowers brought the nose of the lifeboat gently to the trunk of the tree. Tuxedo held the sack in one hand as he called up to the puma, "Do come down, Casanova. You can't spend the rest of your life up a tree."

The puma shook his head. He wasn't too far up, but he was clinging to the tree, with the claws of his four paws dug into the trunk.

"Don't make me climb up there," Tuxedo said in a stern voice. "You know gorillas are much better than pumas at climbing trees."

Casanova looked down at the beasts below him. He squeezed his eyes shut and made a sour face. Then he started to lower himself down the tree trunk and into the sack that Tuxedo held open for him.

"If he escapes from the sack, we can ask that famous question," said Tuxedo.

"And what famous question is that?" asked Edgar, rolling his eyes because he knew what was coming.

"Why, don't you know?" replied Tuxedo, starting to chuckle at his own joke. "'Who let the cat out of the bag?'"

*W*ith the capture of Casanova and his transport to a secure cabin on the *Iffy Queen*, there remained only the return of Captain Blighwater from Maison de Bufo Bufo before the *Iffy Queen* could start down the river again and make its way to AC City. To everyone's surprise, Pegleg wasn't waiting for his captain.

Maison de Bufo Bufo

"We can pick him up on our way back," said Pegleg.

"Do you suppose he's lost his way in the swamp?' asked Max.

"Well, if he did, the toads and 'gators stand a better chance of finding him than we do," Pegleg explained. "So, now it's full-speed-ahead!"

Chapter Nine

Meanwhile, in the Desert...

*W*hile the critters on the *Iffy Queen* had been busy with their labors and adventures, Wil and Harold had started out that day picking a careful route to Highway One. Though they couldn't drive much faster than a fast walk, they were lucky in avoiding anything impossible to drive across. Finally, they drove onto the pavement of the highway. Carefully and slowly, Harold increased his speed. As he approached fifty-five miles per hour, he asked Wil, "What do you think the speed limit is for this stretch of road?"

"It's an emergency, so we can go fast," said Wil.

"Gee, I don't know," said Harold.

"It doesn't matter, anyhow. There's the town up ahead."

A billboard announced the entrance to the city:

Welcome to

TURKEY-BURGER VULTUREVILLE!

It's not toe-foolish to love our great tofu.

"We need to ask someone if they've seen the Pumettes," said Wil.

To the eyes of the canines, Turkey-Burger Vultureville looked a bit odd. To start with, every home had two or more cactus statues in the front yard. The young canines couldn't know yet how the cacti were important to village life. In the mornings, the vultures sat on the

limbs of the cactus with outstretched wings, gazing around at the others in their community doing the same thing. It was just something they had always enjoyed.

The center of town looked pretty normal, though. Harold parked the car across from the town square. He and Wil got out and walked across the street to a small booth in the plaza. A sign above the booth read:

INFORMATION
FREE to VISITORS
A dime to locals,
who should know better

Wil knocked on the booth's closed window.

"Up here, young canines," said a vulture perched on the booth's roof. He had his wings stretched out. "Ohh, that sun feels good. Anyway, what can I do you for?"

"We need some information...," began Wil.

"So far, so good," said the vulture. "You've come to the right place."

"…about three pumas," continued Wil. "They might have passed through town sometime this morning."

"Ahh, yes. In the wee hours of the morning, they did. I know all about it. 'Three pumas,' I said to myself. 'That's noteworthy.' So I took note. Why, just the fact of pumas in our fair city is noteworthy, so I definitely took note. Yes, there were three of them. That's a fact, and a fact is information."

"Do you know where they are now?" asked Wil.

The vulture lowered his wings and sighed. "I do not have that information, I am truly sorry to say. Not a clue."

"Do you know which way they went?" asked Wil.

"Now that, I am glad to tell you, I *do* know. That is information I can supply to your inquiring minds. That way." The vulture pointed with one wing. "And, I didn't see this myself, but Mildred told me she had seen the pumas, all three of them, at the used car lot. It's probably true — why would she lie? So, that's information, also. Right?"

"Thanks," said Wil as he turned to leave.

"Excuse me," said Harold, "I was wondering. You're Turkey Vultures, aren't you? But you eat tofu, not turkeys, don't you? So… "

"So why are we called what we are? Well, even before the Great Conversion, we had stopped eating carrion — you know — dead animals lying in the dirt. I mean, really, would you want to eat something like that? So we started eating turkey burgers. I mean, we already

106

had the 'turkey' name, so turkey burgers made a lot of sense."

"Aah, and then after the Conversion," continued Harold, "you switched to tofu turkey burgers. Sounds tasty to me, but if you never did eat turkeys in particular, why, for gosh sakes, were you called Turkey Vultures?"

Hearing this question seemed to make the vulture sad. "Some critters thought," he said, "and still do think, that our heads — and this is just their opinion, not a fact, not information — that our heads look the same as... turkey heads."

After a quick "Oh, I see" nod, Wil and Harold said good-bye to the poor

A Turkey Vulture, close-up

bird, got back into Harold's car, and drove off in the direction the vulture had pointed.

The used car lot was on the main road out of town, so it wasn't hard to find. They parked the car and walked onto the lot. A very pretty black-and-white Border Collie smiled broadly and hurried to greet them.

"Welcome. Come right in. Always more than glad to serve a fellow canine."

As they walked toward her, Harold passed alongside a shiny and well-waxed car. He stuck out his paw to feel its smoothness. Immediately the Border Collie snapped at his paw and snarled, "Don't touch. That's mine. Leave it alone."

Surprised — almost shocked, really — Harold withdrew his paw. Wil whispered in his ear, "Never touch anything belonging to a Border Collie, and especially never play kissy face with one."

"So what can I do for you canines? In the market for a newish car? Yours, you must admit, looks a little rough," she said. She was smiling again as if nothing had happened.

"We just want to know if you've seen three pumas this morning."

"I certainly did. They didn't have much money. One of them thought she did, but it turned out there was nothing in her bag but a bunch of metal washers. Imagine that. Anyway, what money and jewels they did have, or were willing to part with, could only buy them a motorcycle. Did they ever look funny riding away! The three of them piled on that one little 500cc motorcycle."

"Which way did they go?" asked Wil.

"That way," she said, as she pointed down the highway. "Toward AC City."

"How long ago did they leave?" asked Harold.

"Just about 30 minutes ago," she answered.

"With the three of them on the motorcycle, do you figure the motorcycle's top speed is about 60 miles per hour?" asked Harold while writing something down on a notepad.

"Yes, that sounds about right," she answered.

"Our car's top speed is 100." said Wil.

"Then you'll probably catch up with them. You can do the math," said the Border Collie.

"I'm doing it now," said Harold without looking up.

Wil stared at him for a few seconds. "You know, Harold, by the time you finish your calculations, they'll be even farther away."

"Right, I'd better factor in an estimate of how long it's going to take to do these figures. Let's say…" said Harold.

"Factor in us going right now," said Wil as he ran back to the car.

Harold stopped his figuring and ran after Wil, who was already opening a car door. Harold fired up the engine and made it roar. This time he didn't let it idle down, but put it into gear, and with a squeal of the tires, they started down the road. Soon they saw a sign:

SPEED LIMIT
100 MPH

Before long, Harold had the car up to 90.

"I figure 90 miles per hour is a pretty good speed for this road," he said. "There's no one on it but us right now, but someone might come along. Hoo doggies, did you ever see such a straight road?"

The highway did stretch out into the far distance as straight as a ribbon pulled tight. No other cars could be seen in either direction, and no intersecting roads. The land was flat and wide open.

"Yeah, the land around here is totally flat, no matter which way you look," said Wil.

"Yep, everything's flat," said Harold, "The land, the rocks, the brush."

"Let's keep an eye out for any signs that a vehicle pulled off the highway," said Wil as the desert whizzed by. "They might think Captain Machina is searching for them. I heard pumas are desert creatures. Maybe they know a hiding place out here."

Harold and Wil cross the desert, searching for Renée.

"Can't see how any creature could hide from eagle eyes in this desert," said Harold.

They drove on in silence for several minutes. Pretty much at the same time, each of them saw something far away in the distance. As they approached, they could see it was a creature. When they were about a mile away, they both could tell it was a puma standing by the side of the road. A few seconds after that, they were both certain it was Renée. Harold slowed the car to stop just in front of her and off the pavement of the highway. He and Wil got out and walked up to her.

"Have you come to rescue me, or are you two working for the captain now?" asked Renée.

"We know it wasn't you who stole Captain Blighwater's money," said Wil. "We came because Theena was worried about you."

"Yep," said Harold. "We're more the rescue types."

"Can you give this puma a lift into town?" she asked.

"To AC City? Sure can. Hop in," said Harold.

Renée climbed into the car and sat between the two canines.

I knew it was a good idea to put in that third seatbelt, Harold thought as he started the engine and stuck his left arm out the window (to signal that he was about to drive back onto the highway). Once on the road, he slowly accelerated to 65 miles per hour.

"Theena told me that this is a race car," said Renée.

"Yep, sure is," answered Harold.

111

"I think she's asking why we're only doing 65," said Wil.

"The emergency is over," said Harold.

"But don't you want to catch up with the twins?" asked Renée.

"Naah. Mr. HG and Mr. L. Lobo told us just to see if we could find you, and to make sure you were okay," said Wil. "Now that we found you, we just need to get to the racetrack."

As they drove down the highway, Renée explained how Céline had dumped her halfway across the desert to punish her for giving back the captain's money. She told them the twins probably planned to hide out in the big city, but that she was through with them, and from now on she would sing solo, or maybe team up with Tuxedo.

The two canines told her about the cars they owned and what work was involved in customizing a car. Just to be polite, she pretended to be interested.

"Look! Do you see that?" asked Harold. He pointed to five round objects floating above the horizon far ahead of them.

The balloons captured their attention, being the only round things on or above that totally flat desert (except for the sun above, of course, a few clouds, and, oh yeah, also the wheels beneath them). When the large and colorful balloons were floating almost directly above them, Harold pulled over to the side of the road. The three got out of the car and craned their necks

The famous Flying Squirrels drift overhead and wave to the travelers below.

until their eyes looked straight up. Squirrels looked down at them from the balloon baskets and waved.

"Those must be the famous Flying Squirrels I've heard so much about," said Harold.

"I've heard of them, too," said Wil. "But I've always thought they flew on their own — you know, gliding from tree to tree."

"Nope, you can see that they fly in groups, and in balloons," said Harold.

"Look. They dropped something. It's a little parachute," said Renée.

113

They walked across the sandy desert dirt until they stood underneath the parachute as it gently floated down. Harold reached up a paw to catch the little package. He read aloud the words printed on it:

Know You're Nuts
A new book
by the Flying Squirrels

"Hey, wait a doggone minute. That's an insult!"

"Open the package," suggested Wil.

Harold did so, and pulled out a walnut with a label attached. It read:

The walnut. It's delicious,
but very hard to open
without a nutcracker.

"Buy our book: *Know You're Nuts!*" shouted down a squirrel from the balloon directly overhead.

"Why would I buy a book from someone who doesn't know the difference between *Your* and *You're*?" said Harold, and he shook his head.

Chapter Ten

Good Times in All Critters City

After a couple of hours more in the desert, the highway reached the ocean and turned north. Neither Wil nor Harold had ever seen an ocean before. It amazed them both, but only Harold said it aloud: "Look! Oh my gosh! It's the ocean! It's so, so big!"

Wil felt the same, but he didn't want to seem like a know-nothing never-been-anywhere critter in front of Renée, so he just nodded his head and said nothing about the ocean's immense size or brilliant color.

Along the ocean, signs of civilization showed themselves: beach-front vacation homes, billboards advertising just about everything under the sun that was to be found ahead in AC City, and sometimes a gas station or a roadside café. The racetrack wasn't in AC City itself, but just shy of it, in a little beachside community called Black Dog Beach. The three in the car knew they were getting close when they spied Black Schnauzers racing along the beach.

"What in the doggone world are those things?" asked Harold.

"Schnauzers," replied Wil.

"No, I mean those little vehicles they're driving," said Harold.

"Hmm, I don't know. They kind of look like really small cars, but without auto bodies," said Wil.

"They're called dune buggies," said Renée. "I've seen them in the desert, too. Those little dogs sure have a blast racing around in them."

Indeed, the Schnauzers were having a blast. Highway One ran along the sands of the beach, and sometimes tall sand dunes, empty of vegetation, stood between the road and the ocean. The Schnauzers flew up and down the dunes with reckless abandon. When the little dune buggies came close enough to the highway, the three in the car could see the dogs, their heads thrown back, laughing and shouting and having a great time.

Of course, such fun-loving and adventurous little dogs soon noticed Harold's unusual car. A caravan of them began racing alongside. Harold slowed down a bit so the little dogs could inspect his new type of race car.

"Hoot, mon," called out a Schnauzer. "What would you be calling a fine vehicle such as that?"

"It's a race car. I built it myself," yelled Harold out his window.

"Would you be planning on taking it to the race track, laddie?" asked the Schnauzer.

"Sure would be," replied Harold.

"Why, then, follow us. We'll gladly show you how to get there."

On the way to the Schnauzer town, the three noticed a sign:

WELCOME TO

BLACK DOG BEACH

Home to Mostly Black Schnauzers and a few Scotty dogs

Harold read the sign aloud and then wondered, "How come that Schnauzer talked like a Scotty dog?"

Wil didn't seem interested, and Renée just shook her head and smiled. You see, Harold was a bit unusual in the way he wondered at the behavior of other critters. Most of the animals just accepted the fact that different types of critters behave in different ways. But not Harold. That kind of question always set his mind to wondering, and who knows, with all that he learned about Turkey Vultures and Flying Squirrels and who knows what else, maybe he would write a book about it someday. But today he had to sign up for a race.

They followed the dune buggies off the highway and toward some grandstands and, of course, the race track — a one-mile oval with a golf course in the middle. As soon as he parked the car, Harold walked across the race track pavement and up to the edge of the golf course.

Out on the greens of the golf course were Scotty dogs — playing golf, of course. But even more of those little Scotties drove crazily about in golf carts than actually got out to hit a ball. Indeed, the sport the way they played it seemed more like a golf cart destruction derby. Carts everywhere crashed into one another and Harold could hear the drivers yelling.

"Aye, McClellan, you're a poor excuse for a golfer," yelled one.

"And would *you* be the judge of *me* — seeing as how you can't drive a cart *or* a ball?" yelled the other.

Harold heard Wil call his name, so he turned away from the golf and the destruction derby, and hurried back over to his car, which had drawn quite a crowd of critters. In the center of that crowd, Wil and Renée were talking to a Black Schnauzer with a clipboard.

"This be your fearsome machine, then?" the Black Schnauzer asked Harold. "Well, I can't be saying that the car is bonnie, but would you be wanting to take a couple of practice laps?"

The track manager

"Sure, I don't mind if I do," replied Harold, smiling broadly. He climbed behind the steering wheel and fired up the engine. The fierce noise made the other racers and the track manager move out of his way.

118

Harold put the car into gear and let the clutch out. The rear wheels spun, and smoke poured out behind the tires as if they were on fire. The car jetted forward and Harold sped it around the track.

His second lap seemed even faster than the first. No one knew for sure, because the track manager had forgotten to start his stopwatch. But the other racers stared, wide-eyed with wonder. Harold coasted the car into the pit area.

"Hoot, mon," said the track manager. "That is one blazing fast car you got there. Might as well give you the trophy now."

But he didn't, of course. There's more to racing cars than just being fast — not much more, but there *is* more. Harold thanked the track manager for letting him practice. As Wil and Renée climbed in, Harold shut down the engine so he could ask the track manager a quiet question.

"How come you Black Schnauzers talk like Scotty dogs?"

"Aye, it's a peculiar thing," the track manager replied. "Seeing as how the wee town was founded by us Black Schnauzers, and how only a few Scotty dogs have moved in over the years. You see, the way of it is, you let in even so much as just one Scotty and pretty soon you'll be drinking like a Scotty, then you'll be thinking like a Scotty, and then, before you know it, you'll be talking like a Scotty."

"Gosh, well, what do ya know. Thanks," said Harold. "By the way, what do Scotty dogs drink?"

"Butterscotch soda, of course," replied the track manager.

A Scotty dog

"You'll be in the third race," he continued, "after the Schnauzers and the pigs have their races. Be here early, because there'll be a fair number of city beasties oot and aboot."

As they drove into the downtown area of AC City, they did see a fair number of beasties. Crowding the sidewalks, critters of all sorts were out, hurrying about their business. But although most were in a big-city hurry, some paused to stop and stare at Harold's car.

"Did you ever see so many different types of animals?" asked Harold, Then, seeing Renée smile, about to answer, he said, "Well, you must have, I guess."

"Yep, I must've seen them all," said Renée. "You can drop me off at that building up ahead. The puma elders have an office there, and I need to tell them I had nothing to do with any stealing and scheming. That was all Casanova and his sisters' doing."

"What do you think will happen to them?" asked Wil.

"Oh, well, the elders will probably find them sooner or later and give them a good talking to, maybe exile them to the desert."

"I don't think I'd like that one bit," said Harold, "our elders yelling at us. Nope, I'm going to stick to the straight and narrow path."

"Except tomorrow," said Wil. "You'll be going around in circles on the track."

They let Renée out and said their good-byes. She made them promise to give Theena a big hug for her, and to come see her sing. She was sure to get a job soon. Maybe even at the car show.

"What'll we do now?" asked Harold.

"Let's go find the hotel," replied Wil. "We can tell them the rest of the Hound's Glenn critters will be arriving sooner or later."

"Do you think they got off that sandbar?" asked Harold.

"I don't know. I sure hope so," said Wil. "Mr. L. Lobo will be awfully disappointed if he misses the car show."

The two teens drove around the big city, and by and by they found the hotel where the grown-ups had made reservations. It was near the beach, and as much as they wanted to walk along the ocean, they decided to drive across town to the riverboat port and look for the *Iffy Queen*. There, on an empty dock, they waited until the sun began to make long shadows. Once again they got out of the car, stood at the edge of the dock, and looked across the bay, searching for any sign of the steamboat.

"Hey, do you see something like smoke way out there across the bay?" asked Wil.

"Yeah, I kind of do. Think it might be smoke from the *Iffy Queen's* smokestacks?"

A pelican who worked at the shipping office came over and asked, "You young canines waiting for the old *Iffy Queen*? What do you say I take a short flight over that way?"

She took off and soon was soaring high in the middle of the bay. Harold and Wil could just barely see the large bird in the darkening sky. Toward the far end of the bay, she glided into a wide U-turn, and then she flew straight back to the dock. Before she landed, she shouted down to them, "Yep. It's her alright."

About an hour after sunset, the *Iffy Queen* finally came up alongside the dock. From the second deck, the young ones, the two fathers, and Tuxedo waved and shouted hello to the two teens onshore. As they offloaded Numero Uno, everyone joyfully told of their adventures. Maybe in all that excitement not everyone heard everything, but all were deeply happy to be together at last in AC City.

By the time the two cars arrived at the beach hotel, the four young ones could barely keep their eyes open. It had been a long and exciting day for them, and not even the fascinating sound of waves crashing on the beach could tempt them away from their warm and cozy hotel-room beds.

$\mathcal{T}$he next morning, as soon as they woke up, the canines from Hound's Glenn dashed outside and to the edge of the ocean. As much as Mr. HG and Mr. L. Lobo delighted in walking across the sand and breathing in the clean sea air, they kept an eye on the time.

"Time to go eat breakfast," called out Mr. HG.

After they all had eaten a good meal, they piled into the two cars. Mr. L. Lobo followed Harold and Wil to the track. Having followed the advice of the track manager to get there early, they arrived in plenty of time to find good seats in the stands.

The first race, Black Schnauzers in their dune buggies, caused much excitement and entertainment. But the second race…Well, it didn't seem much like a race at all. Even before it started, the young ones especially had doubts.

"Look! It's the pigs from Big Pig City," Max shouted.

"Are they going to race their roundy cars?" asked Theena.

"And look, they're carrying trays of something," said NicNac.

Three pigs climbed into each roundy car — one in front to drive and two in back to drink tea and eat donuts. When the race flag dropped, the cars slowly drove down the track. Before they reached the first turn, much of the crowd in the grandstands had drifted off to find snacks and drinks of their own. The two teens took their leave to get Harold's car ready for the race. Mr. L. Lobo went off to do a little prep work on Numero Uno.

"Dad, what's the point of this race?" asked Edgar.

"I think the point of it is to not spill their tea," said Mr. HG. "See. That pink car in the middle was slowly being cut off in the turn. The blue car behind him had to brake, and now the pigs are getting out to clean up the mess in the back seat."

By the time the roundy cars came out of the final turn (and they only did one lap), just two cars seemed to be "racing" toward the finish line. The others had parked here and there to wipe up tea spills and vacuum up donut crumbs. The track manager announced the winner over the loudspeakers. A few pigs in the audience oinked. The last of the roundy cars vacated the track, and everyone returned to their seats to await the start of the third and final race.

Chapter Eleven

The Race and All the Rest

*I*t was an odd collection of cars at the starting line. There were five unmodified Too Tall cars, a truck without its bed, a couple of roundy cars (but not driven by pigs), and Harold's amazing creation. Harold's engine made the most noise.

The race flag dropped and all of the Hound's Glenn eyes followed Harold's car as it flashed by the stands and rocketed to the first turn. They had to turn their heads back toward the starting line to see who was

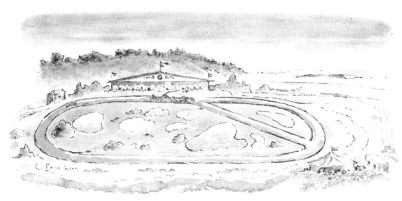

Harold rockets into the first turn, way ahead of the other eight cars.

second. By the time the rest of the racers came out of the first turn, Harold had flown through the second. The Hound's Glenn crowd cheered wildly. Everyone else sat in stunned silence. Over the loudspeakers the race announcers, a pair of goats, expressed to the crowd their own amazement.

"That is one amazingly hot car," the first announcer, Stu, said. "Just what kind of car is it?"

"I'm not sure," said the second announcer, Chet. "But I think it says 'ROD' on the driver's door. It must be a Rod car."

"Well," replied Stu, "That certainly is a hot Rod."

Everyone in the stands watched Harold as he roared into the first turn again. Suddenly, on the race track's far side, everyone noticed a Scotty dog in his golf cart attempting to leave the golf course. He seemed completely unaware of Harold coming around the turn, about to accelerate down the straight-away. Harold, in order to avoid hitting him, swerved violently. His car went into a spin, almost flipping over.

The Scotty golfer jumped out of his cart and raced over to Harold's backward-facing car. He waved a golf club and shouted curses that, fortunately, the young ones in the stands couldn't hear. Other golf carts came onto the track, and more angry Scotties joined the first in waving golf clubs and cursing.

"Oh-oh," said Stu. "It looks like our Hound's Glenn hot Rod racer doesn't know about our track's golf cart priority rule."

"That's right, Stu. The Scotties know race drivers always have to give the right of way to the golf carts," said Chet. "But they've never encountered a car as fast as this one. If they had, that Scotty probably wouldn't have entered the track. It looks like the officials have raised the golfer's caution flag."

"But look, Stu! The other racers are sneaking by that mess and lining up on the other side of it."

"They sure are. It's not a nice thing to do, but you know the rules, Chet."

"As a matter of fact, Stu, I don't. I've never seen the rule book."

"Neither have I, but no matter…Now all the racers except the hot Rod are lined up and ready to go. The Rod is starting to turn around and trying to line up with the others, but they won't let him in. The caution flag is down, and the line of cars is moving, but still they won't let the hot Rod get through the line."

The Hound's Glenn canines watched all this with sadness and disbelief. Mr. HG felt like shaking an angry paw at the race officials, and giving them some of his best, man-oh-man curses, but not in front of the young ones.

"Dad, if they do that for nine more laps, Harold will lose for sure. But who in the line is going to win?" asked Edgar.

"No one, I guess," said Mr. HG.

"Maybe every racer in that line of cars will share first place, and only Harold will lose," suggested NicNac.

"Let's go ask the officials," said Max.

The young ones hurried down from the grandstand in search of the track manager. Not that there was much need for hurrying. In order to maintain their line of cars blocking the hot Rod, Harold's competitors had to drive slow and steady.

Max was the first to spot the track manager, the Black Schnauzer with the clipboard. The young ones gathered in front of him. Edgar put the question to him: "Who's going to win if all the racers except Harold cross the finish line at the same time?"

"Hmm, that's a fair bit of a question," said the track manager. "Let me confer with my flag official."

He turned to the flag official and they whispered back and forth for a few seconds. Then both nodded their muzzles and the track manager said, "Nobody wins, because we only have one trophy. They might've thought they'd be sharing it, but we'll not be paying extra to have everyone's name inscribed on it. So we're just going to say no one wins."

"That's too bad," said Edgar. "Especially since everyone here paid to see a race, and if no one wins, it's not really a race. They'll probably want their money back."

Hearing this put a frown on the muzzle of the Black Schnauzer. He turned to the flag official and for a few more seconds they whispered back and forth. Then the track manager wrote something on a piece of paper, which he folded and handed to Edgar.

"Would you be so kind, laddie, as to give this to the announcers?"

Edgar took it and ran up toward the announcers' booth. The others followed close behind him. They burst into the booth, startling both Chet and Stu, who had been napping, their eyes shut, their elbows on the table, and their paws propping up their heads. Shaking himself awake, Chet took the note from Edgar's paws and, after silently reading it, turned on his microphone.

"Exciting news, Stu. It looks like the officials have found the rule book."

"Well, that's good news, Chet. So, what's the ruling?"

"In case of an eight-car tie, the tying racers have to refund one-third of the day's ticket sales."

"Ouch, Chet. That's going to cost each of those eight in line a tidy sum of money."

"A very tidy sum, indeed, Stu. But not the hot Rod driver. He won't have to pay a thing."

"Lucky for him, Chet, it's in the rule book."

"And I was beginning to think they were just making up the rules as we went along."

Of course, the eight racers in the line blocking Harold heard the announcers saying this over the loudspeakers, and so each of those eight began speeding up a bit, trying to avoid an eight-car tie. Some drew ahead of the others, and this gave Harold a chance to weave between the other racers, move up to the head of the pack, and then pull far ahead.

129

He and the rest of the racers had only one more lap to go when a Scotty dog, returning from The 19th Hole, walked unsteadily onto the track. He looked over at the approaching hot Rod and froze.

"Uh-oh, Chet. It looks like that golfer has had a wee bit too much Butterscotch soda."

Harold braked his car violently hard. It screeched to a stop, just inches from the terrified Scotty. Harold got out of the hot Rod and came over to see if the little dog was okay. But the Scotty couldn't speak or move a muscle, so Harold picked him up and carried him over to his Scotty friends on the golf course. They cheered mightily at this act of selfless kindness.

Unfortunately, three other racers zoomed by the stopped hot Rod before Harold could climb back in and take off in a roar. He didn't catch up with the first of them until the last turn of the oval. The hot Rod shot out of that turn on the outside of the last of the three ahead of him. His engine roared and he passed the second racer. Just before the one racer still ahead of him reached the finish line, the hot Rod pulled ahead.

"The hot Rod wins!" shouted Stu.

"He who crosses the finish line first, wins. We all know that rule," said Chet.

The Hound's Glenn crowd raced down the grandstand stairs and into the area for drivers and mechanics. Harold climbed out of the car to be hugged by his father and brother. The rest of the Hound's Glenn canines shouted his name, "Harold! Harold!

Harold!" But the rest of the crowd shouted what they thought was his name, "Hot Rod! Hot Rod! Hot Rod!"

The track manager came over with the trophy. Harold held it up for all to see. The track manager put into Harold's paws a small purse holding the prize money, and then he called out to the crowd, "To the car show everyone! Harold and his hot Rod will lead the way!"

The Hound's Glenn critters piled back into Harold's hot Rod and Numero Uno, and they led a parade of the race cars from the third race, the tiny dune buggies (and some golf carts), many spectators in their private cars, several buses, and, way in back, the roundy "race" cars from Big Pig City.

The drive to the convention center in downtown AC City became even more of a parade as all sorts of

A parade forms, from the race track to the convention center.

131

critters stopped, stared, and waved at the canines in the two most amazing cars they had ever seen. Some of them joined the parade, marching along with the now slowly moving cars. Just before the parade reached the convention center, Theena spied Tuxedo and then Renée, waving and shouting something she couldn't hear.

*A*t the convention center parking lot, event officials informed Mr. L. Lobo of his assigned space inside the giant hall. Because he and Wil arrived after most all the other contestants, they received a spot back in the corner. This was fine with Mr. L. Lobo. He and Wil needed to wipe off the last of the road dust and put a final polish on every surface that would be inspected by the judges. They even added a little extra polish to the chrome bumpers, making them shine like mirrors.

While Mr. L. Lobo and Wil made Numero Uno's paint glow and gleam, the others explored the maze of cars in the giant exhibit hall. Mr. HG and Harold found some trucks to admire, including one with incredibly large wheels — the inventor called it a "Monster Truck." But the young ones skipped the trucks and tractors and raced straightaway to the strangest car on display.

"Look!" shouted Max. "It's covered with dirt and flowers!"

That was absolutely true. The roundy car, entered by a Big Pig City pig, had been coated with a thick layer of mud, like a cake covered in frosting. And on the mud, the pig had planted daisies and green grass. However, the interior had not a speck of dust. Such are the strange tastes of pigs, who along with hippos, love nothing more than a good clean mud bath.

After seeing the "garden car," well, the young ones didn't think the other cars seemed so odd at all. NicNac raced off to see the motorcycle built for two, with two sets of handlebars and two saddles. They all thought that was a pretty good invention, but then they found the motorcycle with *five* side cars. It had side cars left and right of the driver, and it had a "front car" and a "back car," and topping it off, the inventor, from Leggyville, had mounted one more "car" above the rider. With all those side cars, each long-legged bird could provide rides for five short-legged birds, who couldn't ride motorcycles themselves.

While Max, Theena, Edgar, and NicNac admired the genius of the Leggyville designer, a group of boars walked by. Remembering their frightening encounter with the boars on motorcycles as they left Big Pig City on their previous adventure, the young ones felt relieved to see the boars laughing and smiling.

One of them said to the young ones in a pleasant tone of voice, "Hey, cubbies, don't buy *that* motorcycle. It's for the birds!"

"Well, that's a rude and crude sort of joke," said a familiar voice behind them.

The young ones all turned at once.

"Tuxedo!" they shouted.

"I have some joyful news for all of you," said Tuxedo. "Renée and I will be entertaining you on the return voyage."

All four young ones smiled.

"Mr. Tuxedo, do you know where this address is?" asked NicNac. "I need to go over there and ask Uncle Fang to pay back my pop."

"I'm certain it can be found," replied Tuxedo. "In fact, why don't I escort you there. I could use a bit of exercise."

"Great. Wait here. I'm going to rub some dirt on my face," said NicNac.

"May I inquire as to the reason for that?" asked Tuxedo.

"Pop says I should look poor when I ask for the money."

"Tut, tut, tut. A dignified manner should prevail on all occasions," said Tuxedo.

When Tuxedo and NicNac returned to the car show, the judges were still walking around inspecting all the cars and motorcycles. A large crowd surrounded Numero Uno, and Mr. L. Lobo was hurriedly taking down names and addresses of the critters eager to buy a customized car.

"Hey, NicNac," said Max. "Did your uncle pay you back?"

"He sure did," answered NicNac. "Tuxedo knocked on the door and took off his top hat, and when Uncle Fang opened the door, he took all the money out of his wallet and put it in the hat."

The judges finished their inspection. The crowd grew quiet as the judges came onto the stage and stood behind the microphones. Theena held her breath, but had to draw in air again when she heard a judge announce, "For the prettiest four-wheeled flower garden, we award first prize to..."

It was hard for Theena and the other Hound's Glenn canines to wait patiently for all the other categories to receive their prizes: the hardest motorcycle to drive down the road; the truck with the biggest wheels; the car with the most useless stuff in its trunk. And then finally they heard, "And, now, the moment you've all been waiting for: the Grand Prize for the most exceptional, the most beautiful automobile. We award the Grand Prize to..."

Of course, we all know who won that Grand Prize. Theena and Mr. L. Lobo proudly accepted the large silver chalice.

$\mathcal{T}$he next morning Theena and Harold carried the trophies aboard the *Iffy Queen*. From an upper deck, the Hound's Glenn canines watched as the river otters

loaded the two prize-winning cars back onboard for
the return trip to River Otter City. When everyone
had boarded, and with the cargo secured, Pegleg let
the steam whistle blast out to announce the boat's
departure. He steered the *Iffy Queen* away from the
dock and out into the bay, heading for the mouth of
the river. At the back of the boat and on the top deck,
the Hound's Glenn canines stood at the railing getting a
last look at AC City.

Coming from behind them, a familiar voice said,
"Well done, canines of Hound's Glenn. Well done,
indeed."

They all turned to face Tuxedo.

"So tell me, you young ones. What was the one most
amazing thing you saw during this trip?" he asked.

"The giant toads
riding on the backs of
the 'gators," said Edgar.

"Ah, yes. The
beauty of the lanterns
gliding along in the
darkness of the swamp
— that was certainly an
unforgettable image."

"Those steam engine
furnaces on the *Iffy
Queen*, and the bears
stoking the really hot

fires. Those are some
powerful engines," said Max.

"They certainly are,"
said Tuxedo. "What about
you, Theena?"

"Well, it was all so
wonderful, but I think I'll
remember the critters of
AC City the most. I mean
the way all the different
kinds of animals got along with one another — that
was wonderful to see."

"Indeed it was. I'd
almost forgotten what
it's like to see that for
the first time," said
Tuxedo. "And NicNac,
what impressed you the
most?"

"The steamboat and
the whole river. And
capturing Casanova
Cugat in the swamp. And
Harold's race and just
how boy-oh-boy big the
convention center was.
And the look on Uncle
Fang's face when he
answered the door."

137

"Well, that's certainly a richness of memories for such a short time," said Tuxedo.

"Mr. Tuxedo, what's more — a tidy sum of money, or a mess of dollars?" asked NicNac.

"Hmm, that's an interesting question," said Tuxedo. "But I'd have to say, 'a tidy sum' because... You know, I can't think of a punch line for that. Wait a minute, how about: 'Because a clean business makes not for a mess but for a tidy sum of money.'"

None of the Hound's Glenn canines laughed or even giggled, although they did smile politely. That didn't seem to bother Tuxedo, who hurried on to say, "The music will be much better: Renée will be singing and I will be playing the piano."

While the others took one last look at AC City and the bit of ocean they could see through the bay's entrance, Tuxedo sat down in a deck chair to read the newspaper. On the front page, there was a photo of Numero Uno underneath the headline, "HG Wolf Wins with Amazing Car!" The second headline read, "Hot Rod Wins the Race!" and underneath the photo of a smiling Harold accepting the trophy, the article started with, "Not only did Harold's hot Rod win the race, but Harold also saved the life of a Scotty dog when..."

Tuxedo knew the story, so he turned the page. An inside article explained how four young canines from Hound's Glenn had rescued the *Iffy Queen* from a sandbar. But Tuxedo already knew about that also, because, as we know, he had been there.

The next article to catch his eye had a drawing of a blimpish sort of airship. The caption explained, "Professor Edna Mae Chienne's new invention is designed to fly her and her crew most anywhere the pilot wants to go."

"Anywhere?" said Tuxedo to himself. "Now, *that* is interesting…"

But there would be time enough later for that adventure. Right now he had better find Renée and rehearse this evening's performance.

About the Author

Tonton Jim was born in Corinto, Nicaragua. When he was three years old, he moved to Santa Barbara, California, where his paternal grandparents lived. After a childhood enriched with books, comics, and animated cartoons, he attended San Diego State University, where he earned a degree in Finance. He worked awhile in the reconciliation department of a brokerage service, then left the corporate world and taught elementary school for several years in Oakland, California, mostly fourth grade. He now lives near Santa Barbara once again — fortunately, in a house with a portal to Hound's Glenn. *Harold and the Hot Rod* is his second novella. It follows *Max and the Lowrider Car*, the first book in the *Hound's Glenn* series.

About the Illustrator

Ed Roxburgh grew up in San Diego, California, where his great granny and great uncle, both landscape painters, inspired and encouraged his early artistic efforts. At school his classmates commissioned drawings of cars and monsters for 25 cents apiece. He won awards for his art as a teenager, and expanded his education at Santa Barbara Fine Arts, Academie Minerva, and UCSD Extension. Roxburgh is also a landscape painter; his work appears in museums and galleries. He has had a career creating scenery for plays, operas, movies, TV series, and even haunted houses. He's also a muralist, working in hotels, restaurants, and private residences. The *Hound's Glenn* series marks the start of his career as **E. Felix Lyon,** illustrator of books. Felix lives in Lemon Grove, California, home of some amazing hot rods and lowrider cars.

About
Max and the Lowrider Car
Hound's Glenn Series • Book One

by Tonton Jim & E. Felix Lyon

Max has an especially creative mind for a wolf cub in the fifth grade. Even so, when his teacher tells him to find something *amazing* to write about in their small town of Hound's Glenn, Max is pretty sure that's impossible. Then he discovers Mr. L. Lobo's auto-body shop and his amazing customized car, Numero Uno. And life changes for Max, his friends, his big brother, and nearly everyone else in the town.

The quest for more cars to customize leads a small mixed band of adventurers (wolves and hounds, pups and grown-ups) on a road trip complete with campfire monster stories, motorcycle-riding wild boars, and an invasion by a townful of very perturbed birds. But don't worry — in the end Max dreams up a way to fix everything.

Available from
amazon.com
barnesandnoble.com
and independent booksellers worldwide
(find one near you at
indiebound.org)

CPSIA information can be obtained at www.ICGtesting.com
Printed in the USA
BVOW11s2207261014

372449BV00001B/1/P

9 780989 329033